D1146645

How The Light Gets In

Clare Fisher

Influx Press, London

Published by Influx Press

The Green House, 49 Green Lanes, London, N16 9BU

www.influxpress.com / @InfluxPress

All rights reserved.

© Clare Fisher, 2018

Copyright of the text rests with the author.

The right of Clare Fisher to be identified as the author of this work has been

asserted by them in accordance with section 77 of the Copyright, Designs and Patents

Act 1988.

This book is in copyright. Subject to statutory exception and to provisions of

relevant collective licensing agreements, no reproduction of any part may take place

without the written permission of Influx Press.

First published 2018. Printed and bound in the UK by Clays Ltd., St Ives plc.

Print ISBN: 978-1-910312-12-4

E-Book ISBN: 978-1-910312-13-1

Edited by Kit Caless

Editorial assistant: Sanya Semakula   Proofreader: Momus Editorial

Cover art and design: Austin Burke

This book is sold subject to the condition that it shall not, by way of trade or

otherwise, be lent, re-sold, hired out, or otherwise circulated without the publisher's

prior consent in any form of binding or cover other than that in which it is published

and without a similar condition including this condition being imposed on the

subsequent purchaser.

LEARNING TO LIVE WITH CRACKS

HOW THE LIGHT GETS BETWEEN YOU AND ME

HOW THE LIGHT GETS OUT

LEARNING TO LIVE WITH CRACKS AGAIN

How The Light Gets In

Clare Fisher

learning to live with cracks

in praise of cracks

For much of my childhood, there was this poem magnetted to the fridge: *blessed are the cracked for they let the light in*. I didn't get it: when I looked in the mirror, I saw no light, no cracks, just smooth pot-bellyish skin. Did this mean I would never know light?

Whenever something bad happened, my mum would read out the poem in a voice high enough to break into the world that lay on the other side of the cracks — the world where the light hid. This other world, I thought, must be the one she went in search of when she meditated behind closed doors, and which glimmered in her eyes every time I returned home from school with a fresh prize.

Prizes! How I loved them! I hungered for them. Dreamt about them. And as I grew, so did the cardboard folder of achievements my mum kept in the red filing cabinet downstairs. There would come a point, I imagined, when some spokesperson from the world of light would say, *stop now*. Enough. It's time to join us in the world where no one even knows what a crack *is*.

The folder got so fat, it wouldn't close, but still no sign of the spokesperson. Worry gnawed the meat off me. I had more prizes than friends, and yet the few that I did have glowed with a light I couldn't see; they didn't seem to care about prizes, and I wanted to ask how they did it, whether they'd charmed the spokesperson out of hiding, but this isn't the kind of thing you can ask your friends when you're fourteen. When I looked in the mirror, I saw nothing: no crack no skin no light — no person at all.

Learning to live with cracks — both my own and other peoples'— will win me no prizes. But I don't care. I've been doing it for years now and it feels like life.

If you mention meditation to my mum, she'll wince. As for the poem, I forget all about it until I'm back in her kitchen, filling her in on my latest adventures — the great thing about my mum is she thinks everything I do is an adventure; the big things and the little things and even the things that aren't really things — when, in the crack between a leaflet telling me to stop the war and another asking me to reconsider the philosophy of movement, I spot those greasy words from long ago: *cracked and blessed*.

textbook burglar

There are a ton of theories out there but I don't read them. Although I did once. I read one and then another and another. I was on the internet and you know how it is: you're half-way through a sentence when you right click a hyperlinked word, which opens a new tab, coaxing you somewhere else, and you go there, and then halfway through the next sentence... Where was I? Oh yeah, so I read all these theories and they pretty much convinced me I was a very bad thing. A long, Latin-sounding problem. Nothing else.

You see there's this bloke. He kind of breaks and enters my head. By anyone else's standards, he fucks things up pretty bad; he rips my clothes, stamps on my tech, pisses all over the bed. Textbook burglar behaviour.

Thing is, I'm so used to it, that if you saw me just after a break-in, you'd think I was a bit tired, or coming down with man-flu. You might wonder why I hadn't come out in a while, or why, when I came, I drank but didn't speak, not until you pushed me and pushed me and so I forced open my jaw and the words that came out were blurred — like they were coming from way under the water. Then you'd forget. And I don't blame you: everyone has their own private break-ins to deal with.

It's only when I've finally bothered to sweep and scrub and tidy up; to throw out the broken stuff and go out in search of new stuff; only when I've been running and boxing and fake-laughing and talking even though I've nothing to say and don't believe I ever will but I do it anyway because you've got to start somewhere — only then do I see how bad it was.

And that's the moment I reach out my hand, only to find that no matter how good everything else looks, you're not here to share it with.

You're not here any more.

And so I sit by the window, on the lookout. This time, I'll catch him. I'll catch him before he takes anything more from me.

never mind the gap

Between the you who bought the train ticket in your pocket and the you who is reading this, is the gap.

Now stop reading.
Close your eyes.
Breathe in in in and ooouuuut.
Can you feel it? The gap, I mean.

Well the gap is here, and wafting through it is the you who, whilst buying your second best friend a celebratory you've-just-got-yet-another-promotion-drink read, on the narrow grubby screen of your phone, the email thanking you for your application to the position of Executive Assistant but that it was felt — not by the sunken-cheeked man who interviewed you, but by the universe, in general — that you were *not quite right* for the role.

Dragging its feet through the gap is the you who rang your grandma even though the thought of ringing your grandma made you want to sneeze; this you rubs shoulders with the you who found that, even though you had to shout every word into the receiver so your grandma could hear, even though it was almost impossible to understand her spit-saturated words, by the time you hung up, the heat from your listening ear was spilling right down to your heart.

Slumped at the bottom of the gap is the you who looks out of the window on the journey for which the only proof is the receipt long since chewed by the washing machine. This is the you who's struck by how strange and ordinary it is that you're whizzing past life after pebbled-dashed life; how each is as sprawling and unique and unknowable as your own, and yet, every house is encased in the same slim layer of frost. This is the you that hungers to stare until you've imagined each and every life whole; it's squashed out of the frame by the you who scrolls your Facebook newsfeed, jabbing the screen even though the train is now in a tunnel and — *he's dead, Jim!* — the page just won't load.

Before he was Slip, he was Shorty. He was Clumsy, he was Midget, he was one of Year Seven's seven dwarfs. He was the Year Seven the Year Nines only had to look at, and the dinner money would fall from his blazer pockets. He was the boy who stayed in the school library until it closed to minimise the amount of time spent playing with the cling film wrapper his mum left over his dinner whilst she was at work. He was a loser; just like anyone else.

Slip has nothing to do with that boy. Slip, although only two inches taller, is the kind of kid Year Elevens nod at in the corridor, whilst Year Eights and Nines apologise if he rushes them in the lunch queue. Somehow, a rumour started that he stuffs his socks with blades; when people ask, is it true, he just smiles and shrugs, as if it might be (it's not).

Slip has a swagger that all the Year Sevens copy. When Slip shows teachers an 'early home' pass signed by his 'mum,' they nod and look away, breathing out deeply as he says, *safe!* And swaggers out of their classroom.

Slip hangs with his crew until 9:10 p.m, leaving him just enough time to run home, chuck the cling-filmed dinner over the balcony, scatter some pens and school books around the table, and climb into bed before Mum stomps through the door, muttering and sighing about whatever it is she has to mutter and sigh about.

Slip has been caught snoozing in class three times in the past week, but it's alright because he's not the boy he was before and so he styles it out, kissing his teeth, ruffling his shoulders and saying, loud enough that the whole class can't help but hear: 'And WHAT? I was *just chillin'*. *Just chillin'*.'

And now, any time a teacher tells anyone in that class off, they say: '*just chillin'*, *just chillin'*,' and everyone laughs, whilst he sucks in his smile, not wanting anyone to hear this boom-boom-boom in his chest that tells him he is king.

When his eyes *are* open, it's harder and harder to focus on the weird-ass symbols and the weird-ass equations ands the weird-ass teachers; his mind keeps wandering back to those six sweet hours with his boys — the only time he's *properly* home. He makes out like they are up to Big Man gangsta shit, but mostly, mostly, they sit around on walls and bikes, gassing and laughing and, when they can be arsed, teefing crisps and chocolate from the corner shop. They drink Coke and chat about girls and GTA and COD. Then there's the chicken: at some point in the evening, there is always chicken. *Don't eat too much*, the Big Guys tell him. *We need you small*. Slip wants to ask why but just laughs and nods. *Stay that size and your time will come. Trust.*

The only similarity between Slip and Shorty is this itch of fear, which slides somewhere between his skin and his hoody. Slip has no trouble ignoring this itch until he's squeezing through a stranger's dog flap, a big brown envelope tucked into his pants, a knife in his sock, heart racing, eyes seeing only that Slip's time is up: the boy is turning into something else.

the genius

Her mind is bursting with great ideas but other people have always thought of them first. Not only have these other people thought of them; they have often turned them into real things you can buy in shops or on Amazon. This is why she is stuck folding ties in a TM Lewin in the interminably draft-ridden Leeds train station. Her only customers are businessmen pissed off because their train back to London is delayed (there are a lot of delays at this station). The managers do not allow her to wear gloves because gloves (they claim) would damage the ties, which means her hands are permanently dry and numb, which means she has trouble tapping her ideas into her smartphone at the end of her shifts, which is another reason she is stuck here, trying to smile at businessmen whose eyes don't bother to hide the fact that they hold her personally responsible for the fact that they, important businessmen with important businesses waiting for them back in London, are still stuck here too.

mistakes

Will be made.

And sometimes, you will make them.

You will press the button or fill out the form or turn the corner or write the word or say the sentence or open the door that everyone agrees is wrong.

Some of these times, someone or two or three or many, many people will find you out. Some may even post a photo of said mistake, or of the pain they have suffered as a result of said mistake, on social media. Other people may RT this photo or christen it with a hashtag, which may or may not catch on.

Other people may shrug and say it's okay, they didn't really care whether you saw them in their concert anyway, and you may nod and say thank you, acting as if you don't know that this other person is squirrelling away this mistake of yours for some barren moment in the future, in which your argument about another mistake of yours you are yet to make, suddenly runs out of fuel.

But don't worry. Because most of the time, the mistake will be made by a human being who is not you. And you will be the one who is tweeting a photo of your recycling bin Which Has Still Not Been Emptied For Two Weeks In A Row If You Think This Is What GOOD PEOPLE Pay CounCil TAX For. You will be the righteous in your capitalised certainty that the wrong things are all outside.

But not always.

Not always.

Because mistake will be mad e, and somtimes

Sometimes

The person making them

Will be

You.

the thing about sheep

Our parents compensated for the fact that we were growing up in a city of over seven million people and God knows how many million tons of concrete by driving us out to the country ever other weekend. We'd spend the morning crawling through traffic to reach the M25; lunch would be eaten from a tupperware somewhere along the M25, and even though the whole point of packing tupperware was to avoid the over-priced service stations, we would be so close to a) wetting ourselves, and b) killing each other that my parents had no choice but to stop.

There would inevitably be some disaster in the country: our father would trip over a stone and twist his ankle; our mother would drop her wedding ring in a cow pat; I would climb up a tree and find myself too anxious to come down. If you ever have the misfortune to have dinner with my parents, you will no doubt hear at least one of these *hilarious* anecdotes.

However. What sticks in my mind about these misadventures is the sheep and how angry my brother got when he saw them. 'Do they mind just sitting outside all day?' he'd ask my dad and my dad would tell him that no, of course they didn't, they were sheep and they didn't *mind* anything — they just were. My brother's face would wrinkle and warp and then he'd pound his fist against a delicate stone wall and my mum would shout at him and he'd shout at her for shouting at him and then my dad would shout at them for shouting at each other and so on and so forth until we decided it was time to go home. This happened every time we ventured out and yet it inevitably got over-shadowed by whatever drama was particular to that day.

When we got too old to be forced into a hot Volvo on a Saturday morning, my parents did everything they could to sign us up for Duke of Edinburgh and whatever other outdoorsy activities our school offered. I, a straight-A student, a goody two-shoes and, as my brother would never let me forget, my parents' favourite, *loved* these trips; I even won an Award for leading my group to safety through a storm when one of the party was injured and the other having what I now know to be a panic attack. As for my brother, he *hated* them; teachers would ring my parents complaining that he wouldn't take part, he was winding up the other boys, etc., etc., and the final straw was when he was brought home early and suspended from school for smoking weed when — in the words of the teacher who broke the news to my dad — he should have been preparing dinner for his teammates. It was then decided that the great outdoors and my brother should have nothing more to do with each other; my parents can now laugh about it, given he has 'settled down' since then and now lives in a cottage so remote it cannot be reached in certain months.

I was always sure there was more to it than that, however, it was only the other day that I got around to asking him. We were, as it happens, getting stoned (my idea, not his).

'What was it about the sheep?' I asked. 'Why did they make you so angry?'

We laughed and laughed, but I knew, even as he was wiping tears from his cheek with the edge of my Moroccan throw, that he knew exactly what I was talking about.

'I was jealous. They could be who they *were*. Do what they needed to do. Whereas we were forced to spend our whole fucking weekend in Dad's car.'

This set us off again.

'But of course they thought it was grass I hated or something. Those Duke of Edinburgh trips only made me more sure: being a human *sucked*. It was slavery. And being forced to trudge through the New Forest with a load of other humans who didn't even get weighed down by manky food and some manky tent, that was so much worse. So much worse.'

'I've always thought being a human was... alright,' I admitted.

'Yeah,' he said. 'No shit.'

Where laughter would have been a few minutes ago, now there was silence. 'So what about you now? The whole human thing? You reckon it's... okay?' He didn't know it — Okay, he most probably did know it but we liked to pretend he had no idea — but we worried about him, out there, with so few humans and so little concrete.

'Yeah,' he said, smiling like he was in on some secret he would never share with me, 'it's alright. But most of the time, even now, talking to you, I just pretend I'm a sheep.'

the insomniac

He is always falling asleep in restaurants and in the cinema
and in armchairs at his relatives' houses because — he
always points out crossly when they wake him up and tell
him that he has been dribbling or murmuring or snoring —
he can never get any sleep.

what women want

What do women want? What should they want? What do *we*
want? Because who are we if not them, these women whose
desire is suddenly a problem of public discourse.

Do we want one lover or two? A man or a woman? A
single or a return? Brown bread or white or are we gluten
free? Do we want curvier curves? Do we want a thigh gap?

Recently I've wanted to eat a whole box of macaroons:
gift-wrapped with ribbons and tissue paper, every last
crumb for my own mouth. I've wanted to gather up all
the world's stuff and share it out equally (which means no
macaroons and definitely no gift-wrap). I've wanted to lie
down in the middle of my office in the middle of the day and
sleep. I've wanted for some manageable disaster to occur
so that I can walk away from the unbearably boring person
who's talking to me without seeming rude. I've wanted to
live in London and Leeds and Paris and New York and a
tranquil mountain village in a country I've never heard of.
I've also wanted dry socks, a less bitchy internal monologue,
a less snorty next-door neighbour on the train. I've wanted
to cross the road right now and not when the lights change;
I've wanted a plug for my dying iPhone.

Now I just want to hold onto this feeling that I'm here

and it's good that I'm here and that here shakes you up, here holds you down; here is confusing and strange and dark and difficult — *here* is never quite ready but, nevertheless, good. And so here I am, hoarding it, boxing it up, ready for me to unwrap and gorge on the next time I feel low and flat and unplugged.

dark places to watch out for [1]

That look in your eye you hope no one — most especially not your son — will ever see.

The silence which crusts around the woman who slaps her child on the bus.

Revs on a Friday night when already, you don't want to be there, and then some idiot spills raspberry vodka shots down your top and shouts as if this is your fault, and then some other idiot gropes your arse and the friends of the other idiot tell everyone you love it, and so, when — finally! — you fight your way back to the people who, if not exactly your friends, are not as idiotic as the other people in here, you think the fluttering in your chest means you're happy.

Those times when your daughter rings you up demanding to know why you ignored her in the pasta aisle of the supermarket and, rather than admit that your senses are not as sharp as they once were, you tell her that choosing between penne, spaghetti and something-something-li is a very important choice indeed. *More important than your own daughter?* she asks. And, your heart breaking yet again, you snap, *Yes*.

The bottom of the bin — any bin will do.

The mostly-forgotten late nineties/early noughties girl band, Atomic Kitten; their songs find their way into your ears at the precise moments when you are likely to cry.

The days when you hate everyone, everyone — including all the ones who are not yet born. In fact, *especially* those ones.

the neurotic

Every time someone refers to her as chilled out, she grins and blushes and shrugs and makes some self-deprecating comment to deflect the attention which, if it were to rest on her any longer, would surely reveal that she is not, in the truth she keeps buttoned under her pretty fitted blouse, in the least chilled-out; she is neurotic. She is so neurotic about not appearing neurotic that she is unable to fall asleep until she has figured out how to arrange the next day so that, from the outside, it appears scattered and empty and random, but from this inside place into which she will never allow anyone else, it is unarguably under control.

Over 100 people have been asked what scares them but the results are unknown.

(An additional 19 people claimed not to be scared of anything. Two said they were scared of cheese but otherwise they felt perfectly safe and comfortable in the world).

One male, age bracket 21-25, white other, sexual orientation prefer not to say, said that the purpose of light was so he could see the food in his fridge at night. He did not say whether or not he was joking.

One person who left all identifying characteristics blank, wrote in capital letters that did not fit in any of the boxes WHY ARE YOU WASTING ALL MY AND YOUR AND EVERYONE ELSE'S LIFE WITH THESE DUMB QUESTIONS WHY DON'T YOU GO OUTSIDE AND GET A LIFE OR LIKE A BIG MAC OR SOMETHINK.

She did not use any question marks.

Seven people answered no to every question, even when no was not one of the preset answers.

@whatyalookingat tweeted:
We #know what UR #UpTo #suspicious
#whatdotheytakemefor #lol

It has been concluded that another questionnaire is needed before any conclusions can be reached.

how the light gets into the city

the guardian of travellers

With bags under their arms, bags on their backs and bags under their eyes, the travellers come to him. They stumble, trudge and tumble towards the sign over his head which reads, in letters way wider than his shoulders, **Victoria Coach Station WELCOME INFORMATION.**

Where is Victoria Train Station is it long long way from coach where is Underground? How do I find Queen Hotel? Which Metro line for M&M shop? Where Kew Garden? Where Angus Steak House? Where is passport? Where is JOB where is my brother I tell my brother meet me Victoria Coach Station where is LOVE?

If he is waiting for one of the others to return from their break so he can go on his and his was meant to start ten minutes ago; if he is bursting for a piss or a custard cream or a Nescafé Gold or a scroll of his Facebook; if he is desperate for a few minutes alone so he can finally shake that last argument with his girlfriend out of his head; if a fortnight of night shifts and afternoon shifts and some other dark thing he can't name, are weighing him down; if the security guys have just dragged away four drunk lads who kept calling him gaaaay and spitting at his face, he will shrug. He will stare, his face no more communicative than the dirty tiled floors, and point at the rack of leaflets by the taxi rank.

If, however, his belly is warm with custard creams and Nescafé Gold, he will smile (but not too widely due to the brown splodges on his teeth which are growing every day). He may, if his cup of Nescafé Gold was particularly strong, stand up. *Left, left, left right,* he'll say. When the travellers' faces knot with worry, he lays his hands flat on the chin-high desk that divides him from them and makes the noise his mother used to make when he would seize up with terror at imaginary monsters.

I know these streets like the back of my hand. Pull your case towards Costa, turn right, cross towards the white boards painted with buildings they're still yet to build. Breathe. Say hi to the pigeons, but not too loud, mind: they may get excited and crap on you. If they do, don't worry; your hotel is the big silver building glinting at you from the other side of the topless buses on the other side of the road.

With every traveller comes an opportunity to rediscover the city, never mind if some or sometimes all of the details are what most people would call 'made up'. *Ride the 44 bus to the second-to-last stop and you will find the job of a lifetime. Don't miss the cronuts in Giuseppe's Deli, West Brompton Road. The gargoyles on St Anthony's Parish Church in Camberwell are deliciously gruesome, and the pub round the corner does a decent roast, too. There are elephants in Trafalgar Square tonight — one night only! There are raves in every second basement in Mitcham. There are stars painted onto the toilet floor in the dentists at Kennington.* Some would say he is mean; others would say he is mad. He'd say he's just pulling out the city that is already there — the real city, below the tarmacked surface. (Although he can admit he has done more than the statutory maximum number of night shifts this month.)

The lost travellers nod and blink, unable to absorb more than a few familiar words — 'and', 'if', 'road'. And yet they smile; they loosen their grips on their front-to-back-packs. *Thank you*, they say, even if they're too tired to speak.

As he watches them melt into the 3 a.m. floodlit darkness, he knows he's given them at least one good thing to write/text/email/Skype home about. If he can be the one good thing in a fellow human being's long, bad, difficult, day, he's glad.

But this is not how he spends the night shift, oh no; he spends most of it watching the creatures who waft through the automatic doors, so skinny and scrappy and hollow-eyed, he often fails to see them until they are folded into some corner, limbs tight as origami. The security guards don't see them either, or if they do, they don't move them on; these people have lost too much muscle and fat and money and bags on whatever kind of journey it is that they've been on: you can't be a threat to anyone if you're not really here. He wishes they would come over and ask him. Ask him anything. Ask him why. Ask him how. Ask him if he can make it better. They never do, though. They never do.

me-time

You know what your problem is? You need some Me-Time.
Such was the advice of Holly — the far too smiley Holistic
Wellness Coach with whom HR insisted, because I'd had
more than three sick days off in the past six months, I spend
an entire 45 minutes of my life.

Take yourself on a date! she squealed.

I hate dates.

Buy yourself a cupcake!

Not a fan of cupcakes.

By this point, Holly was looking far from well. Okay, she
said, her eyes darting about the windowless meeting room
in search of an answer, *How about a nice, relaxing walk?*

Now, walking is something I *do* like to do. The Firm are
forever posting me to new and different cities, and whilst
my colleagues are curled in their hotel beds, chomping
microwaved room service food, I am bounding as far away
from those towers of fold-away ironing boards, as my
cardiovascular capacity allows.

All I want is to be like those clever literary men who,
whether they are stumbling upon the soaring spires of
York Minster, a derelict mill in Bradford, a modernist water
garden in the Barbican, or the humungous Westfield which

swamps Derby's 'city centre', are overcome with thoughts so Profound, they last for pages and pages, and could not possibly be interrupted by anything so frivolous as, say, a paragraph break or a full stop.

But no sooner is The Hotel — regardless of which city I'm in, it's always the same hotel — out of sight, and this me time-space is filled by someone else. I'm halfway across Blackfriars Bridge, halfway towards The Ultimate Profound Thought, when some woman thrusts a camera into my hand and asks will I take a photo please oh thanks. (This, by the way, is before the age of selfie sticks.) I take photo and she shows it to the man who is either her brother or her lover, and the man says I've chosen an interesting angle, am I into photography, and I'm about to say no when the woman says, Yeah but like no offence, she's cut off the top of the shard, so would you, like, take it again? Yeah but isn't this meant to be about us, not The Shard? says the man. I don't give a shit about The Shard. *I shit on the Shard!* The woman raises her eyebrows and says, You couldn't shit on The Shard it's too high, you *idiot!* Then she pushes the camera into my hands and says, I'm really sorry but like no offence can you take it again anyway? Cheers. So I take it again, and again, and again, and then they insist they take me for a drink, it's only fair, and of course, of course, I say yes.

And just as we squeeze into a Georgian pub so cramped, they end up shouting their strange and twisted not-quite-love story in my ear. The next time I'm in Leicester, with my lunch break sucked up by a market stall holder who tells me, in between attempts to flog plastic bowls of soggy grapes for £1, that he's the reincarnation of Richard III. In Edinburgh it's a human statue whose tears bore fleshy streaks in his silver skin. The Edinburgh to Leeds train? A woman in a long flowery skirt who, when her phone won't work, leans across the table and tells me how her husband just won't deal with his mother's death, if she brings it up he acts as if she, she tells me, between blowing her nose on her skirt, is, through the act of saying it, killing her husband's mother all over again. Leeds to London: a couple arguing over whether they should follow the advice of *Natural Fertility in the Twenty-First Century or Conception in the Digital Age*. London to Leeds: a young man whose eyes fill me with more sorrow than these stories put together. Leeds again, and my nocturnal explorations of its medieval ginnels and Victorian towpaths are invariably truncated by a woman, always the same woman and yet always a different one, who tells me I've come too far; this place is too dark and dangerous for a girl like me, and when I ask what kind of girl they think that is, they plunge into the story of whatever awful thing happened or didn't happen or almost happened to them, it happened right here or just over there or right where that tree is, and whatever the story, I stay until the end, which is always something to the effect of, *It was the lowest point in my life so who knows why I keep coming back!* You could say the same for me. You could ask why it's at the turning point of someone else's story that I feel the most real — the most me.

Aha, so you paper over your own flaws with other people! Holly exclaimed, somewhere towards the beginning of this story. I was exactly the same …

Rumour has it that Holly is paid as much for one consultation as we're paid for a week of interminable meetings. Although I don't feel unwell, I'm pretty sure I'd feel well*er* if they'd paid all that money straight to me. I'd have used it to book a holiday to some place to which this firm has not and would never send me, say a village way up in the Andes or the Himalayas; I'd have flown out alone and flown back with a heart-full of other peoples' stories — stories far stranger and stronger than the titbits I glean in these skimpy pockets of time when I'm not at work, and which would make me feel, by the time my head hits the pillow each night, a little less alone.

But who cares what I'd prefer? Not HR. The feedback form contained three 1cm-squared options only: 'Extremely Helpful', 'Fairly Helpful' and 'Helpful.' I stared at these boxes through the myriad twists and turns of Holly's story, which was so long, our 45 minutes was up before she reached what she termed 'the OMG moment'. By this point, I was so desperate to leave, I didn't even tick the fingernail-sized box, which is the only kind of story you're allowed to tell around here.

helping elbow

People talk about helping hands but they never talk about helping elbows. Well maybe no one ever elbowed anyone the way she elbowed me. I'm not saying '*she*' to be rude: I never learned her name. It was the bus stop outside the Corn Exchange; they call it a *shelter* but it don't shelter you from much — not from the pee or the wind or the rain or anything that may or may not be going on inside you and sometimes, sometimes, you wonder like is there something dirty and wrong with the fact that you even exist.

Anyway that's exactly how I felt when she elbowed me in the tit — right in the squishiest middle of my tit, and I said, 'What do you think you're doing you clumsy bitch? This world ain't just for you.'

She was so gobsmacked, she dropped her Harvey Nicks bag; tiny silver balls rolled all over the pavement. I reckoned they was pearls or summat. I picked one up, rolled it between my thumb and finger. It was all oily and I said so.

That's when she stared over my shoulder like behind it was some window to some other place (not just the scratched-up out-of-date bus timetable) and said, 'It's bubble *baaarth*. It's for my sister-in-law. I thought it would make her like me but it won't. She will never like me, and to be honest, I don't really like her, and I guess that's alright. Anyway, I'm sorry. I hope I didn't hurt you.'

We didn't become best mates; nothing like that.

She walked off, her bubble baths rolled and rolled until people stepped on them, until more people stepped on chips and then stepped on the ones that was left; by the time my bus bothered to show up, there was no shine on the pavement that anyone else could see. But as the bus rattled past the huge Dalek building, I looked down at the dirty fingers at the end of the hands at the end of the person that way too many people had said was no good and I could see it. I could see the shine alright. I still can.

things smartphones make you less likely to do when alone, in a public place

Stare at every passing stranger who is a similar size/shape/ sex/style to the one you are waiting for in case they are indeed the one you are waiting for.

Stare at strangers who are a completely different size/ shape/sex/style to the one you are waiting for because you do not want to admit to yourself that the one you are waiting for is still not here. Eavesdrop.

Read all visible adverts, free newspapers, leaflets, warning signs, safety advice and strangers' books, newspapers and diaries; because words, even boring ones, have the magical ability to transport you away from the larger boredom of standing on a cold platform, waiting for a train which a very silly, mostly hidden but nevertheless substantial part of you, hopes will never come.

Ask strangers for the time or directions to such-and-such address or to the nearest coffee shop or whether they know the area and can recommend a coffee shop, you don't mind a walk if there is excellent coffee at the end of it, oh, and cake — cake is always good.

Pick up that novel whose characters do so many annoying things and have such annoyingly similar names that you have to keep flipping back to the introduction to remind yourself why so many people who know so much about literature think it is worth reading in the first place.

Ring your friend to find out about their exotic holiday because you are about to start planning an exotic holiday and could do with some advice (no option of scrolling through their holiday photos on Facebook).

Work out where you are by looking up, down, around and around, trying left, trying right, trying straight ahead, even though you can only hope this is the direction in which you are meant to be headed.

Having stared at all visible billboards, including one for a pantomime that finished running two weeks ago and whose overly made-up actors' over-grins make you feel a bit sick, not to mention the diet planner of the woman standing next to you, having checked all available clocks and timetables and watches, you are forced to admit that the one you are waiting for is not going to come; not only that, but the one hasn't even bothered to let you know that he or she is not bothering to come; formless sounds escape your mouth as you finally admit to yourself that yes, you are pissed off.

fried chicken

When people ask me how did I do it, I usually use big words like 'faith' and 'trust' and even 'perseverance'. But tonight is about shining a light on things worth shining a light on and so in this spirit I can reveal that the real answer is fried chicken.

Yes, that's right: fried chicken.

Biologically speaking it's more 'fried' than 'chicken', it stinks and is a shocker to the vital organs and even to the not-so-vital ones. But back then, when loss was pushing me over the edge of time and way down deep to some anti-time in some anti-place where nothing and no one could touch me, not even the brightest stick of sun, I did occasionally make it from the bed to the window.

It was a grimy window; I had to press my forehead right up against the glass to see out. And what was out there but the red and yellow orbs of Dixy's Fried Chicken. The fluorescent hamburger 'Os' of Mahmood's. The unforgiving strip lighting of the shops themselves, showing up every pimple and wrinkle in every figure that flocked in empty-handed and out, weighed down with cardboard boxes whose outer skins were printed with pictures of flames which, I remembered from my Being Properly Alive days, were always slightly pixelated.

My Being Properly Alive days! As the air warmed and I was forced to sleep with the window open, they floated in on waves of grease. Looking forward to things, for example: big things — like my big sister's wedding — and small things, like M&S 2 meals for £10 (and a bottle of red) on a Monday night. The pain of no longer having such things mingled with the pleasure of the thing in its original.

Eventually, my limbs began to twitch, and lying in bed all night and all day got, well… Boring. Then the moment came when I had no choice but to slip my feet into my trainers and pad across the road to those too-bright lights.

Dixy's fluorescent logo was an unambiguous YES. I stood beneath it and craned back my head, dismayed to note that the huge plastic letters were dotted with the corpses of dead flies: the NO wrapped up within the YES and A Sign that I should go back into the stale shell of myself right now, for what was the point, when a voice called: 'What do you want?'

A man stood in Dixy's propped-open door, mopping crusted ketchup from the floor tiles. A tiny paper hat was attached to his wavy black hair with a kirby grip; that he'd put so much care and attention into one small detail, it moved me; I edged towards him.

'Erm, I'm not sure.'

'Why don't you come in and take a look? We've got some great deals on, and I'm not just saying that because it's my job, honest.'

It was a long time since anyone had given me such uncomplicated instructions and I was grateful. I tried to tiptoe around his mop but he told me to walk right over it — 'I can just do it again, it doesn't matter!' — and so I did and a few moments later I was leaning my elbows on the (decidedly un-mopped) counter. Chicken Wings Dulux. Chicken Dulux. Chicken King Family. Chicken King Supreme. Having been presented with an exciting menu of nothing or nothing for months, my heart whimpered at all this choice. My eyes misted up and I let out one of those weird nervous sneeze-coughs.

The girl behind the counter flashed me a knowing smile as if to say 'Don't worry, I've seen it all before and more.' But she didn't actually say this. What she actually said was: 'If you can't choose, make sure you've answered the basic questions. Like, are you hungry or just peckish? Or are you properly starving? Hangry, perhaps? Got the munchies? The drunkies? Or do you just want to eat something for the sake of it?'

Hunger: it had stalked out of my life a long time ago. But maybe this was one of those situations where it was better to lie. 'Hungry,' I said. 'I'm just, erm, *normal hungry*.'

'Normal hungry? In that case, I'd suggest a Chicken Wings Dulux.'

'Okay.'

'Have you been here long?' I asked. Yes, this was me. Believing in the existence of other human lives strongly enough to actually ask a question.

'You mean in this shop? Or in Leeds? Or on this earth?'

'Ermm…'

'Sorry. I get like this sometimes. I'm doing a PhD in behavioural psychology with nutritional sciences.'

'Aha. So this is research?'

'I like to tell myself that. Mainly, it pays the bills now I've run out of my loan.'

I wanted to know more. I wanted, more alarmingly, to tell her my story. Was it a story? Maybe it was a story. Maybe fried chicken was merely the gateway drug to radio call-ins, magazine problem pages and Jeremy Kyle. But as she shoved the hot little cardboard box across the counter, her eyes glazed, I got the message: she was done for the night. Fair enough.

It wasn't as if I had a long journey home, but I sat at a high window stool as if I did. Outside, there was a bus stop, and although Leeds has no night buses, a man was sat there, jiggling up and down to his iPod. A rogue crisp packet scuttling across the tarmac. I counted 47 different things to see before my eyes settled on my own grubby window.

'Closing in twenty minutes.'

Get on with it. Okay. Opening the cardboard lid — whose printed flames were, disappointingly, of a far higher quality than the ones I remembered — I breathed in the grease and the *je ne sais quoi* that croons 'eat meee, eat meee'! (Or it could be 'MSGGGG! MSGGGG!') My stomach rumbled. Not that I was hungry — I would never be hungry ever again — but I could perhaps nibble. One chip disappeared into my mouth. Then another. Then I realised I'd forgotten to get any ketchup, and chips without ketchup were a crime against humanity, and — 'Ketchup!' I yelled, and the conscientious mopper swiftly deposited a handful of sachets by my side, and I ripped them open, hands shaking, jaw chomping, because my body was now awake, at silly-AM it was ravenous for a whole new day, and there was nothing I could do to stop it going at that chicken, so rubbery and delicious in my former vegetarian's mouth; oh how terrifying, to want so much so fast!

And that was it. That was how it began.

this city knows you better than you think

Your smile may be Facebook-ready and you may have already distilled this moment into an epically RTable tweet but that doesn't stop you from leaking yourself all over this city — the parts of yourself that are not in the least RTable.

The city, for example, knows about that time you spent the whole journey from Camden Town to Clapham South fantasising about your boss then feeling unbearably guilty about this because: 1. Your boss isn't in any way attractive, 2. Your boss has this gross habit of licking his teeth between sentences, and 3. Your boss always talks to you about watching *Game of Thrones* with his kids even though you have repeatedly told him that you don't watch *Game of Thrones* and you don't like kids. You sweated all this into the long rubber arm of the escalator, which you grabbed all the way up to ground level, your mouth agape at the strangers who marched up the stairs, hands-free, unafraid to fall.

Another thing the city knows is how much you hate your girlfriend's dad: the city captures the skin that flakes off your scalp, which itches and itches and itches, every time he 'treats' you to dinner in that expensive Soho steak restaurant. (You don't particularly like steak.)

It knows that sometimes, whilst starting *War and Peace* for the sixteenth time, you just want to be famous. It knows that on the rare occasion you walk down a street and don't see the flicker of another human, you pick your nose — whether or not it needs picking. It knows when you jump at the mice under the tube tracks. It knows when your thoughts (or your Facebook feed) whisk you away to a world that is much easier than this one; this is when taxis almost run you over, and you jump and scream and stumble back onto the pavement, your pores pumping stress hormones into the air. It even knows when you walk across Millennium Bridge, knotting a path between tourists who are pausing and posing to express the am-I-really-here-yes-I-am simple joy that you, at this rare sunny moment on a rainy November afternoon, are able to breathe in, box up and keep.

Yes, this city is always watching. Counting. Absorbing. Your life is slipping, splitting, ripping, tearing, drip drop dripping into bits so small and spread out that when you reach out to catch yourself, your fingers waggle through empty air, and you wish for something — anything — to which you can cling.

The city is dealing with your enquiry as soon as possible but it won't answer back. It won't help.

For a moment, tears prickle at the corners of your eyes and you wonder whether this is it: whether this city is finally defeating you. Whether, by this time next year, you'll be moving to St Albans or Milton Keynes. Then you notice the fruit seller, and how picturesque he looks, tightening his striped awning, looking this way and that, oblivious to the mirrored towers that block out the sky on all sides. Phone out, and — you look around, a little embarrassed, but no one's watching, fuck it — take a quick selfie. And here is your chin-heavy face, accidentally positioned so as to give the impression a bunch of bananas is balancing on your head. You use the last of your 3G uploading it to Facebook, Twitter and Instagram and wait. One buzz, then another and another. At last, you can relax. Yes, you are many things, and this city knows about all of them, but right here, right now, you are are one silly face in a city of eight million people that thirteen other people like.

the truth about beards

The discussion was heated, as discussions of universal significance always are. The matter in question was beards and why every second bloke suddenly had one.

'They didn't happen *suddenly*,' said Greg, pedantic in all matters both beard-related and otherwise. 'Beards take a lot of time and effort. They are like well-behaved dogs.'

Greg, FYI, lives in Homerton with two moody pugs.

'It's a revolt against the New Masculinity,' said Will, who thinks he has a beard but, owing to a genetic predisposition to look forever like a withered teenager, has only lopsided chin fluff. 'It's a desire to return to the fundamentals.'

'What about the women,' I said, being one. 'What do we do when we yearn for the fundamentals? I doubt *me* growing out my beard would go down too well.'

'You've all got the wrong end of the stick,' said Ben. 'And the stick is screaming, capitalism! As with East London and, and,' he flung his arms around at the mismatched ensemble of old cinema seats, sewing machine tables, bar stools and school desks, 'this fucking pub and all the other pubs around London like it, so with beards. A trend gets popular, bang, the dickheads come along and want to make money out of it.'

'Shall I get another round?' asked Will, who hates Ben's anti-capitalist rants as much as the rest of us. 'Same again?'

He nodded at our collection of craft ales, microbrews and, in my case, a G&T garnished with locally sourced mint (probably lopped from the huge bed of it growing in the weed-strewn 'beer garden.').

'If we're not hipsters,' I asked, picking a dead ladybird out of my G&T, 'who are they?'

Ben slammed his brew down on the table, careful to lap up the overspill with his skinny thumb. 'We're not going over this *again*.'

'We just have the same conversation, over and over.'

'We're pissed.'

'We've only had one drink.'

'Two. Three if you count the ones on your roof terrace.'

'You've got a roof terrace! Come on! Admit it! We're hipsters, of a sort. What's wrong with it?' I said.

'What is *it* exactly?'

'No doubt many boring sociology tomes are being composed on MacBook Airs on the balconies of what used to be council estates as we speak.'

The drink leeched our conversation of significance — universal or otherwise. This upset me somewhat, but not sufficiently to stop me drinking. The only other thing I remember from that night is Will, who had been unusually quiet for an unusual length of time, leaping forward — which wasn't very high as he'd been slumped in a granddad armchair — and declaring: 'I've got it. I've cracked the beard question. Everyone in London wants to be different right? They want to be sheep, not goats. What are goats famous for? Beards.'

'They piss on their beards to make them shine,' interjected Greg.

'Yes, thanks for that,' said Will. 'Anyway, ergo, you, I, we all have beards because we want to be goats!'

No one said anything for a moment, and then everyone laughed. Had I suggested another round right away, they'd have begun arguing about something at a comfortable remove from our own lives — whether the *Inherent Vice* film was artistic genius or artistic torture, for example — and the beards would have receded to their rightful position of barely noticeable background detail. Instead, I checked my phone (four new messages in a group Facebook message thread about an event I probably wouldn't be arsed to go to). I was about to leave the thread when Greg poked my thigh and I looked up to see Ben seal this night into Will's cheek — and all of our memories — with an almighty punch.

like, the best night out ever

This night is like the best night ever and you're gonna make sure everyone knows it because to look at some of their faces you'd think they'd forgotten or maybe never known it and this is like the saddest thing in the world, apart from like famines and holocausts and wars and child cancer and stuff, which you don't really want to think about on this, the best night ever, and so you go up to these two guys who you've never met before but what does that matter because isn't it just a stupid rule that you can only talk to people you've already talked to that people made up because their best nights were over and they were bitter and so they were scared to make the whole world their friend like you're doing now, and you tell them: 'Can you see it? My fingers sparkle.'

One guy looks at the other guy and the other guy looks at the first guy and the ground shakes from under you and your ankle goes over the edge of your stiletto and you land in a hairy place, which turns out to be the guy's arms.

'Let's see if they sparkle in my pants,' he says. And suddenly your hand is hot and sticky, your bum is cold on the ground, the sky is more grey than black and the birds — high up in some tree some place that you can't see, the birds are fucking singing.

'There she is! Oi, get off her you perv!' And your friend,

your oldest bestest friend, who you've known since that fateful fight over the best Lego person on the play rug in reception class, is whacking these guys over the head with the stiletto which must have fallen off your foot which no longer has anything to do with you because what even are you?

'Poor babe, you've overdone it again, haven't you? You've got to stop this.' Your oldest bestest friend squishes your head against her chest but it doesn't protect you because what you see as you stumble through the lost stilettos, the abandoned hats, the bent-up earrings and dying glow sticks, are the ugliest scraps of yourself. And to think, you were parading these scraps to strangers not so long ago! And you thought they liked it! You thought they wanted it! This is. This is the. Like. Like the worst.

'What?' says your friend, alerting you to the fact that you have been saying some of this out loud. 'This is like —'

But do you not manage to tell her that this is, like, the worst night ever, because you are retching and retching and yep, still retching, and she is rubbing your back and saying there there, there there, and you want to tell her not to worry because this is what you need, you need to get this whole night out of your system; from now on, you'll be satisfied with okay-ish night after okay-ish night; you must do like the sky and start all over again regardless.

dark places to watch out for [2]

Wet seats, especially on the patterned fabric of tube seats which are designed to fool you into a wet behind for the rest of the day.

The derelict warehouses around the canal, and the darkness in their bellies, and the way their windows, distill the sun and the moon with equal finesse.

The days when you hate everything, *everything*. Including the Self-Service checkouts. *Especially* the Self-Service checkouts.

That strange brown blob floating under Waterloo Bridge. It is probably an old chair, but even so.

The raw purple skin on the homeless woman's hands that you pretend not to see whilst you queue for the cashpoint, fretting over whether to take out £30 or £40.

The black mould that grows under your bedroom windowsill no matter how many times you scrub it off with a toxic spray which is almost certainly worse to sleep next to than the mould.

no one messes with hot pants

You were running from that cheating tranny in Gipton. Or your boyfriend. Or both.

You were curled tight as a fist at the back of the bus, knocking your knees, tap-tap-tapping on the window on which someone who was here before both of us had scratched the word

BOOM!

I was stretched across the two front seats, pretending that the empty aisle between us was soundproof, pretending to read a book about two made-up characters who should be together but for reasons both tragic and ridiculous, were not, or not yet, at this point, a thumb's width away from the end. Your words kept breaking into my ears and into my brain and I was no longer sure whose story was whose.

By the time the bus swung towards the once-glossy Queen's Hotel, you were telling whoever was on the other end of your phone that you couldn't decide between hot pants or a skirt this Saturday, 'because I'm gonna show that bastard I'm not like all the other slags at Yates or whatever he said because I know he said he never said that but he did. I don't remember, who actually remembers what anyone ever said? but it's the kind of thing he *would* say, apart from, he'd say it *worse*, and you wouldn't be able to make out the words he'd be so *fucked*.'

The engine died and the driver cleared his throat in that uniquely passive-aggressive bus-driverly tone that we all know means: *get the fuck off*.

You sprang from your seat and although I wanted to see whether there was any cheating tranny or boyfriend waiting for you outside — I could already imagine him in a wig and Madonna cone boobs — I wanted slightly more to trace the minuscule emotional changes that would have taken place in the lives of these two made-up people by the end of what was a particularly agonisingly teasingly long sentence.

The only reason I could find for choosing this made-up story over yours was that the author had promised me an end, and an end I could feel just the other side of the blurb. Half of me felt guilty, whilst the other half reasoned that you probably wouldn't want me to hear the end of your story, anyway: yours had only spilt into mine by accident.

But when I caught up with you — and about thirty other pairs of tired shoulders — waiting for the loop road to stop looping so you could keep walking or running or bouncing or whatever it is you were really doing, I couldn't help smiling when you said: 'Okay, okay, hot pants then. No one messes with hot pants, not even him, eh?'

shortcuts

Everyone says I'm a right numpty for cutting through the 'Yorkshire Ripper' ginnel every single morning, but what they'll never get into their custard-creamed heads is that for me, a life without shortcuts would be no life at all.

The Yorkshire Ripper didn't even do 'owt in this particular ginnel; the nearest place he did his business is round the back of Morrisons. And no one ever says, *Don't go to Morrisons or the Ripper will get you!* Do they? They're the ones what are numpties, if you ask me.

It were actually Darren who started the Ripper thing. Darren is my youngest son and he'll say anything to get attention, and even though most of what he says is nonsense, he says it in such a way that it's fun and shiny and you can't help but listen. It were one of them Sundays when we went out as a family (rather than stayed in yelling and laughing as a family). We walked past the ginnel, which is so dark and damp you can smell it from the road, it smells like how the bottom of a pond would smell if you drowned, and Darren pointed and said we had to go down there, because he'd been doing about Jack at school and he could tell that this was where Jack lived. 'I'm going to catch him and keep him in at playtime for a whole week and all.' Of course, Jack the

Ripper weren't Yorkshire Ripper, but no one said 'owt; Tom and Megan were egging him on with spooky noises, and we went down there, all laughing and screaming and jumping up and down like a family in the Centre Parcs advert, and apart from when I had to grab Darren to stop him picking up a needle, it was one of the best days out we've had, now that I think of it.

If I didn't shortcut down the ginnel, I tell people, when they start having a go, if I walked all the way over the bypass, I'd miss the bus, wait God knows how long for the next one, then be late for work, which would mean I'd have to stay late, which would mean I'd have to pay for one of them after school clubs, which would mean I mightn't as well bother going to work in the first place. 'A car!' they say. 'What about a car?' But I don't say 'owt because who wants to say that scraping together the cash for a car is about as likely as getting to Centre Parcs?

Thing is, there's this other reason I cut down the ginnel every single morning — a reason I'll never say 'owt about to anyone. You go into the dark and the shadow swallows you up and the stink swallows your nostrils and you're all alone with the drip-drip-drip and the scuttling of mice or rats or whatever the hell lives down there and your heart's beating like the drum in drum-and-bass and not in a good way because it's a Tuesday morning, you're on your way to work, your drum-n-bass days are long since over, you've a house full of kids. *Bricking it*, is what you are. But you don't want to miss the bus so you shuffle on. On and on into the dark, and the railway's rumbling above you, and — splat! Water drips on your head, messing up the 'do you woke up extra early to perfect, but what do you care, you 'ent scared no more, because bang smack in the belly of the ginnel is where you are, more of a tunnel than a ginnel now that you think of it but ginnel is what everyone calls it so ginnel is what it is; there's no light at the end you came from and no light at the end you're going to and here — here is where you stop. It's just you, the dark, and that drip-drip-drip. *Please, Mummy, please…* No letters asking for a £25 deposit for a school trip. No one saying can you photocopy this, oh and this and this and this, can you just stay an extra 20 minutes … No hand on your hip when you 'ent in the mood, no ache between your legs when the mood is all over you but nowhere near him. No nodding and laughing to the hundredth instalment of your sister's un-story about her new garage.

Sometimes I stay so long, I miss the bus and all. I think about missing the next bus, and the bus after that, but then the drum in my chest starts up again, and I think, What if there's no more light? What if I never see Darren's cheeky grin again? And Megan's 'why 'ent tea ready yet?' eyes? And on I stumble to the other side, and by the time I'm out, there's mud all up my tights and I feel like everyone's right, like *I am* a right numpty, because of course the light's been here all along, it's always here, it's just that you're not always in a place where you can see it.

twenty-first century celebrity

Turn right at the lights and left under the road bridge for Richard III. If you're on foot, don't worry: dodging traffic on a dual carriageway and scaling concrete ramps has the medieval levels of danger that Richard would no doubt approve of. If you don't want to see Richard III, tough: you are going to see him whether you want to or not.

It's pretty hard being Richard III these days: he never gets a chance to escape himself. And always the same version of himself: that terrible etching — churned out by some lazy apprentice — some idiot has printed over and over. Richard can't even buy a pint without stumbling over his own ugly mug, blown up big and happy on the wall! Can't get a bargain at the market, either; the vendors insist that the 70p per bowl price is only for the 'peasants'; he, however, must pay the vegetables' weight in gold (never mind if the so-called 'peasant' besides him is scrolling through her smartphone). He has tried explaining that his gold ran out several centuries ago; no one listens.

One chap even grabbed his arm in the street — just outside of Zizzis — and told him to get down off his throne and tell Theresa May what's what. *A throne!* Wouldn't she love one. Although he was perfectly content with his DFS deluxe faux-leather retractable armchair until the chap said that. It is hard to be content with much, in fact, since they dug 'him' up in that car park; he's stopped getting work as a freelance tax accountant owing to all the 'dirt' they dredged up, along with the body, and, after growing delirious with insomnia from the incessant knocking at his door, he has had to rent an apartment at the top of a new development halfway down the canal — of whose existence no one else is, mercifully, aware. He shops online and answers the door to the delivery man in sunglasses and a hat. He keeps getting emails from people claiming to be 'PR experts' but he immediately deletes them: he doesn't know what PR is and nor does he want to. The sensible thing would be to leave Leicester, but he doesn't want to do that, either. No, Richard III is not cut out to be a twenty-first century celebrity.

this city's roaring edge

You are leaning over the railing that protects us from this city's roaring edge; I am eating salad with a plastic spork.

'Can you help me?' you ask, throwing your shoulders as near to the traffic as your bones allow.

Your question coincides with a particularly enthusiastic gust of wind blowing off the rubble-patch that was once the International Pool and which I wish, every time I wipe its gritty off-blow from my eye, still was. It also coincides with a particularly awkward-shaped mouthful of smoked tofu.

'Can you help me get home?'

I want to tell you that there is International Pool graveyard grit in your beard.

I want to ask you where your home is and why you decided to pause and reverse your journey away from it on this flimsy pedestrian bridge that hardly anyone uses and we both know why; our ears are flooded with the racket of people moving, moving, moving.

I want you to know that there was a time when I would have sat down beside you and stayed there until the fear got too much. But I am an adult now, and this is Reality.

'No.'

Some nights, as I am rushing towards the cardboardy

comfort of my Ikea bed, I see you; you are still here, still at the roaring edge, the second to last person I will see today, and I smile at the gap in the railings to the left of your head, knowing that your question is no question, that you know something I, in my salad-munching hyperactivity, may well never learn: how to be still.

under construction

They came with bulldozers and drills, hard hats and high vis and spades. Why they needed the spades when they had bulldozers and drills, the Aslan family had no idea. Toby, the youngest Aslan, claimed he'd seen the bulldozers dig a hole and then the men jump into it and finally the men jump out, their spades glinting with treasure.

'There's no treasure around here,' said Sally, who always referred to herself as the second eldest even though she was also the second youngest.

'They've no idea what they're doing, that's what,' said Tim, who watched the 'boys' (he always referred to them as boys) dig and drill and piss and laugh and scratch their balls and eat sausages and pickles out of jars. As the rest of the family was fighting over whose turn it was to use the bathroom first (they had tried, many times, to put up a rota but despite Mia's best efforts with Excel, it never worked) he pulled his armchair to the window and watched. He refused to go to bed, no matter how much Annie, his wife, coaxed him: 'What's the point?' he said eventually. 'The drills will keep me up, and anyway, it's not like I have to get up in the morning.' Annie half-smiled and turned away as quickly as she could from the strange creature her husband had somehow become.

Every Aslan was kept awake by the drills and the digs and — later — the creak creak creak of the cranes; yet each Aslan watched the Pickle Boys (as practice now dictated they be called) dig up the scrubland and fill it with concrete and steel and mud and — although this was only according to Toby — bones. Sally, on her way to school, noticed playing cards with naked women on them buried in the mud. She felt sorry for those muddy women and promised herself never to let her life get as small and as flat as theirs. When concrete slabs filled the gaps between the steel skeleton, Ash, the eldest, noticed a photo of a family taped to the inside of one of the square holes that would one day be filled with glass. When the walls were two or three times as high as their house, Annie saw that the illustration painted on the edge of the construction site — two and three bed luxury apartments — did not feature their house or their terrace, and that the blank-faced people walking around the two and three bed luxury apartments did not resemble any human beings she had ever seen in her not-so-short life.

'It won't work,' was Tim's daily mantra, even as the towers darkened the — already meagre — dose of light which fell through their front windows. 'They're lost boys. A load of Peter Pans with gherkins. They've no idea what they're doing. I'd be finishing up the job now if *I* was foreman on *that*!' When Tim said things like this, Annie found it impossible not to notice the crescent of milk which had been crusted to his dressing gown for months.

Then, with no warning, the gherkin boys disappeared, along with their diggers and their bulldozers and their high vis and even their spades. Tim said more than he had in months: 'What did I tell you? You can't go about things like that and expect them to work out; things don't work out. And I'd bet money on the fact there was bad money behind it. If I had any!' The other Aslans knew exactly why the not-quite-finished towers meant so much to Tim; they also knew that a joke from him in these post-employment days was a rare and special thing. If he could joke about himself, did this mean they could joke about him? Toby opened his mouth but, in a sudden moment of mother-daughter telepathy, Annie and Sally shook their heads no. Then they laughed. Laughter was good enough. If they kept at it long enough, Tim would see that the person he currently was, was pre whoever he was going to be next, not only post.

'Maybe it's not the end,' said Sally. 'Maybe it's just a pause.'

how the light gets
between you and me

There are a lot of things we don't talk about; mostly, we don't talk about them on Skype. What we do is, we talk about the weather and how it is always better where you are but then the cinema is better where I am, so we're even.

Then.

These gaps.

They spread.

You scratch your nose. I tuck my hair behind my ears for the seventeenth, the eighteenth, the nineteenth time. Somewhere beyond the edge of your webcam, a cat meows.

'That game,' you say, your face flash-flooding with emotion. 'The rocks. Do you remember?'

My hands fill with the bobbly pebbles from the beach where we no longer play. My nostrils crackle with salt, and somewhere between your screen and mine, there soars a seagull.

'You always changed the rules to suit yourself,' I say. 'And you never let me go first.'

'God,' you roll your eyes. 'So this is another thing you can't get over. How much more's to come?'

'It's a whole childhood,' I say. 'You can't digest it all at once.' I close my eyes, not telling you how it comes to me in in jagged hole-ridden pieces as I dive into my local swimming pool, or as I turn on the tap to rinse my mouth of toothpaste and all that crap that grows in your teeth in the night.

'Look at us!'

I open my eyes. You are laughing.

'Just look.'

We rub our noses against the screen. Are we brothers? Are we sisters? Are we lovers, old friends or young worms? Are we soul mates? Are we freaks? Who knows. Who cares. Not me, not now — now that 1.67 thousand miles and two time zones away, we are finally getting to the gritty bottom of *it*.

'It wasn't easy for me, either.' Your words spark through the gap between your lips. I think of the way you used to run out of the kitchen in the middle of dinner, a box of matches in your hand, lighting then throwing as many of them off the cliff as you could — before someone made you stop.

'It was —'

Your mouth is half open, your tongue a dumb red blob in the dark. There are three deep creases in your forehead. Your eyes are stuck forever mid-blink. What's wrong? What happened? Are you there can you hear me was it something I said where are you are you dead?

The screen blanks. Then I hear that blip, blip, blip — the sound submarines would make if they ever tried to communicate underwater — of Skype trying to reconnect.

Six minutes, ten years, three lifetimes and twelve box

sets later, you're moving again: 'I'm back. Don't know what happened then. Weren't you telling me something?'

'No,' I say, 'you were telling me. You were telling me about —'

'I've forgotten,' you say. 'And it was probably something incredibly boring.'

We sigh, knowing that this silence is buzzing as our brains search for excuses, but maybe that's okay; maybe we've come as far as we can.

one woman's love

She pulls out her phone whenever someone mentions love. *Do you love him? But are they still in love? They are SO in love, it's SO cute! It's SO annoying. I love them. I hate them. Are you going to their wedding?* She would rather read a book but pulling a book out of your bag when someone says something boring or annoying isn't socially acceptable whereas pulling out your phone is; if you hold the screen right up to your face you can maintain the fiction that you have something really important and personal to attend to, rather than just, say, the 'live' timetable for a journey you have already taken.

She tells her partner she loves him every day — in the same way her mother told her she loved her every day, when she was growing. Other things she tells her partner every day are whether or not her bus to work was on time and what made her laugh on Facebook and what made her want to hit people in the office.

Despite having spent a greater proportion of her life in a relationship than not in a relationship, she feels that a greater proportion of her 'self' is unknown than known. She does not really believe that she loves or ever has loved or ever will love anyone or anything; people talk about love as if it is this rare and special thing and yet they talk about it so much that it becomes just another word to fling around along with, for example, *cat, ball, fridge* and *bird*. She is now 35 and if she has managed to get this far in life without anyone finding any of this out or even suspecting it, she suspects she will make it to her death in the same way. Sometimes this saddens her and other times it is a tremendous relief. But most of the time she is thinking about whether or not there is milk in the fridge and if there are any films coming out that she wants to see. Most of the time she is happy.

without the dark there would be no you

You! You were made in the dark.

You were made in the dark because I was embarrassed to take my clothes off, and he was embarrassed — well I can't tell you about that, not just yet.

I say 'made' rather than 'conceived' because 'conceived' sounds like the flash of an idea in someone's brain, whereas 'made' sounds closer to what, erm, actually, you know, is.

I know exactly which night you were made on because we hadn't attempted to make anyone for at least a month. Before that, we'd been trying once or twice daily for a year. Your father's mates thought it must be great — to come home from work knowing you were guaranteed a shag. But it was not great. It wasn't even good. It hurt. Sometimes he took so long to come, I'd fall asleep wishing I was doing some other chore — like the washing up, or even, even, the ironing.

You know those military campaigns in the Middle East where the bombs fall and the guns fire and everywhere, everywhere, children are dying, and no one stops to ask why and so on and on they go because they can't remember what they did before this — well, that's exactly what it was like.

It was like that until one day we did stop. He was on top of me; he was squishing my lungs and I said so; he clamboured off. After we'd wiped and washed and dressed ourselves, after we'd switched on the lights and were lying on opposite sides of the bed, him facing the door, me the window, him reading *Freakonomics* for the fourth time, me *One Day* for the third, he said: 'Shall we give up then?' And I, the word a dead weight on my tongue, bursting to jump off, said, 'Yes!'

So for a whole month, instead of fucking, we watched box sets. We got bad seats to a play that left us with dry mouths, creased foreheads and creaking backs. We went for one impromptu walk in the park. We tried out that new tapas place and both agreed we preferred the old one.

We avoided friends with kids to start off with, but so many of our friends had kids that to avoid them was pretty unavoidable after a while, especially when their kids were constantly having birthdays. I hate kids' birthdays. I hate the screaming and the brightly coloured food. I hate the googoos and the gaagaas and the glitter and the Disney themed napkins and the possibility of vomit hanging in the air. I hate having to drink out of tiny plastic cups. I hate how you'll be approaching the nitty-gritty core of the conversation when the person you are talking to suddenly runs.

I hated being at that particular party and yet, I was thrilled to be there; at last, I was able to admit that maybe, maybe it was okay not to have all this — maybe some part of me was relieved. Another bonus was that, being the only non-parents in the room, your father and I had monopoly access to the least disgusting bottle of wine. We hovered around it, concocting wild plans to travel, to set up a boutique business, to learn new languages, meet new people — things we'd never bothered to do in this year of war. Then his foot brushed mine. I kicked him. And so we ended up playing footsie, giggling and blushing — as if we were teenagers, meeting for the first time. Then he grabbed my hand and pulled me upstairs.

Yes, you were made, not only in the dark, but in someone else's bed. (I won't tell you whose because the couple in question wouldn't be too pleased if they found out.) You were made in passion and ignorance; you were made in the fug of alcohol, in the spark of we-shouldn't-be-doing-this-what-if-we-get-caught. When it was over, we lay, sweaty arms on sweaty bellies. He fell asleep but I kept my eyes open, and I noticed that the dark wasn't really the dark; I could make out the shape of his body and he, I realised, must be able to make out mine — he'd probably already seen the bits I didn't want him to see — the bits I didn't like.

***

Over the next nine months, as you grew and grew inside of me, as my body swelled and surged with new life, I forgot to feel embarrassed about it. It was what it was, and often it was hot and slimy; I took to walking around the house naked, in every shade of dark and light. He, I could tell from the way he watched me, he loved it.

***

You were gurgling in the shut-eyed darkness of your own preverbal dreams when I found out why he was so scared of the light; when he climbs into me, he cries. 'I'm sorry,' he said, when I first found out. 'I can't help it.' I'd never seen him cry before; I'd just assumed he didn't need to. 'No need to apologise,' I said. 'At least now I can be sure you're not some sort of tear-less robot.' He laughed then cried then laughed again. Inside me, he shrank then swelled then swelled again. Then we carried on. The light was on the whole time but neither of us commented on this fact; we've stopped caring about such details; you are so rarely asleep that it's all we can do to seize each opportunity as it comes.

things smartphones make you less likely to do when in a private place, with or without other people

See awkward/boring conversations through to their bitter ends because you cannot pretend there is something more important happening on the palm-sized piece of plastic which you angle, carefully, away from the awkward/boring person's line of sight; the only escape routes are those such as feigning a coughing fit or a need for the bathroom which will only lead to further awkwardness/boredom.

Say, 'oh well' when someone mentions a film star whose factual accuracy no one at the table is sure of, and move on, because whether that film star is still alive and if so whether they are married to that embarrassingly bad rap artist whose name, incidentally, no one can remember, is by no means essential to this conversation, which is not awkward or boring, but would become both of these things were everyone to shut up and stare at the person who is staring at their Smartphone, waiting for the page to load so they can verify facts that no one cares about.

Look words up in dictionaries.

Wake up to an alarm clock (rather than Facebook notifying you that today is the birthday of two people to whom you haven't spoken to in years and, now that you think about it, are not sure you have ever spoken to).

Stare out of windows.
Stare at the wall.
Talk to your partner in bed.
Talk to your partner whilst they are cooking the dinner and you are pretending to dust.
Stare at the shrivelled pot plant in the corner which, were it an animal, would no doubt have been rescued by some sort of charity by now.

Prepare for a journey into some public space you have never been to before or have been to but don't remember too well, by printing out, or, if you don't have a printer or your printer is out of paper or ink, by copying the backbone of your Google Map onto the back of an old Council Tax bill, even though you know perfectly well that your markings will bear no resemblance to the real world, but which you fold into your pocket and carry out with you anyway, because being lost with a crappy map in your pocket is better than being lost with no map at all.

Accept that if you want to know something or buy something right now — tough. You will have to wait.

headtorch

The elastic snaps against his head; the torch bobs up and down, down and up, as if it's already out there, running.

'You look crazy,' I tell him. 'Or like you're about to go down a mine.'

While he stoops to tie his laces, I think about his granddad and how he actually did go down mines. I imagine him crawling for miles and miles in the dark, and how, between him and the light, there would be miles and miles of earth and earthworms, and broken crockery and bottles, and decomposing dog shit and banana skins and baby birds that tried to fly out of their nests too soon and so had fallen and died.

Then I remember that his granddad returned to this earth a good deal earlier than he should have done — than he would have done if he hadn't breathed in so much dust so far below ground.

I'm trying to mumble some of this out loud, when he switches on the head torch, blinding me.

'Bye then,' he says. His hand, fluorescent white from days and months and years spent inside, hacking at a keyboard, closes around the door handle.

There is nothing but darkness outside. Nothing but

darkness and the rattle of freight trains along the tracks and the rustle of other things, worse things, that cannot be seen.

'Don't go down to the canal,' I say. 'It's dangerous. Why don't you get up at sunrise and go then.'

He rolls his eyes. 'No one's going to wait in the shadows on the off-chance that they can mug a runner... And for what? All I've got with me are my keys and,' he taps his head torch, 'this. Much more dangerous to run on the street.'

There follows an argument, whose contents I won't bore you with, about the relationship between danger and darkness. Finally he says, 'Look, I don't care if it's a bit dangerous: everything's a bit dangerous. I want to run, I need to run; the dark is not going to stop me.'

He's gone, and I flock to the safest place in our apartment: my laptop and its friendly anaemic glow, in which I can wrap myself — 24 Things You Didn't Know About the Winter; 13 Special Offers to Get You Through the Dark — for the 45 minutes until he scuffles in behind me.

'That was brilliant,' he says, beetroot-cheeked, panting. His head torch pierces my eye. 'I felt so free, so alive. You should come with me next time.'

And maybe I will. Maybe I will follow his bobbing spot of light into the dark. But I'm not going to admit that now. I'm not going to let him win. Instead I frown and shut my eyes. 'Turn that damn thing off. You don't need it now that you're in here.'

the wrong thing

What's wrong? she'd ask, whenever more than three seconds of silence stretched between them. Nothing's *wrong*, he'd reply, his tone rubbing awkwardly against the content of his words. Well something clearly *is*, she'd say. You sound all like, you know, *pissed off*. By this point, she'd be grabbing his arm so hard, her fingers were burrowing through his T-shirt, or, if it was An Occasion, shirt. *Yes* I'm pissed off, he'd say, flapping his arms, as if, he thought, on one of the many occasions he replayed this and every other significant and insignificant moment of their relationship in a neverending quest to decide whether or not to break up, he was trying take off. But he didn't want to take off; he just wanted to dislodge her nails from his skin. I *knew* it! she'd say. I knew as soon as we left the flat that something was wrong. But it isn't! he'd exclaim. It isn't it isn't it isn't. Then why are you so pissed off? I'm pissed off, he'd tell her, because you've ruined a perfectly fine afternoon by asking what's wrong. By now, tears would be trickling down her cheeks. I didn't mean, she'd mumble, to ruin anything. And then he would say sorry, and she would shake her head and wipe her tears and say that she was the one who was sorry, and on they would go, on and on in a spiral of sorries, until one of them spotted a suitable distraction, such as a Two-for-One burger deal or a stupidly cute dog. And just when their bellies were full, when they'd tickled the dog into a stupor, when their cheeks were aching from laughter, when their brains were zinging from having shared every thing they needed to say and every thing they didn't really need to say but said anyway because what was the point of sharing your life with someone if you couldn't just say a thing without worrying whether it or not it was the right one, just when he was beginning to wonder whether everything was, you know, like perfect, that's when she'd grab his arm and ask, What's wrong? Not again, he'd grumble. I can't believe we're doing this *again*. Then he'd turn to hide his smile, for, tangled up in his annoyance, was relief; this was perhaps the only area of his life in which he knew what was coming and it felt unarguably *right*.

dark places to watch out for [3]

Most evenings, at around nine o' clock, you wonder whether you'd be happier living with a dog or a cat or a guinea pig or a hamster or a rabbit or a Komodo dragon or a clan of stick insects or a newt or a chinchilla or even a stuffed dodo, than with a husband.

Even if you bother to clear out your wardrobes and your chest of drawers and those plastic boxes you had to buy from Wilko's to stow the clothes that wouldn't fit in the wardrobes or the chest of drawers, and donated all that you didn't want or need to the worthiest of all charity shops; even in this ideal world where you are far more organised than you actually are, you could not undo all the childhoods and adulthoods which were broken in some, or many, factories faraway, in order to make you these cheap clothes which, even though you have far too much of them, are never quite enough.

Your five-year-old's face when 'baking' a cupcake on the iPad.

The drawer under the bed where you keep the hiking poles, complicated coffee grinder and 'Learn Swedish in Ten Days' DVDs which even your fingernails know will be here long after you have ceased to sleep in this or any other bed.

The days when you love everyone, everyone, even the ones you have never met. Especially the ones you have never met.

unproductive behaviours

From 9 to 5, Monday to Friday, you watch other humans' — wait, no, employees, you must remember to think of them as employees — screens. You watch their screens on your own personal MegaScreen. Whenever one of the screens within your MegaScreen burbles with 'unproductive or borderline unproductive' behaviours, you must click said screen — right click for *borderline*, left click for *unproductive* — thereby registering the log-in identity of this borderline unproductive or unproductive *employee* in the database which your company purchased at no small sum.

Your boss, who likes to remind anyone who will listen — and indeed, anyone who won't — that he was *instrumental* in acquiring this *revolutionary* new technology based on the *latest* scientific principles: 'I'm a big picture person,' he'll say, whilst craning his neck over your shoulder. 'And the big picture is this: you can't put a price on company ethos, no you can't.' He knocks your hand off your mouse and left-clicks over the screen of User MR78, which is plastered with a local news article about a cannabis farm which was busted in the back of the building in which you used to eat Chinese on a Friday lunchtime, back when lunchtime was still a *thing*.

Repeat offenders must attend a 'workplace ethos and personal attitude' workshop, led by none other than your boss. These workshops consist of a four-hour-long PowerPoint, 'created' by your boss, and which he uses his weekend and evenings to update because, 'constant improvement is what it's all about — in work as in life'. Every time you hear his voice, you are overcome with the desire to *de*prove yourself. To rip off your shirt and writhe around on the over-shampooed office carpet like some prehistoric sea creature. But you need this job. And so you only do the prehistoric sea creature act in the dusty room at the back of your mind, which not even your boss can see.

Mostly, you express this desire by *not* doing things, e.g. not clicking the screens of Users ME2 and BJ45 when they engage in a lengthy email exchange as to whether an unknown user they refer to as CrabbyCakes looks fatter this week than she did last week and, having decided she does, whether this is because a) She only makes a big deal of doing the 5:2 diet to make the rest of them feel bad and actually goes home and scoffs Jaffa Cakes, or b) Is she like literally knocked up from U No What Happened With U No Who in the toilets at the back of that club what was it called on that last night out?

Instead of logging this as 'unproductive behaviour', you purposefully return to their screens a few hours later, learning that User BJ45 found Unknown User CrabbyCakes crying in the disabled toilet, but that she wasn't crying about her pregnancy, but about her cat, which had recently died. And she was, literally, like the best cat ever. Users ME2 and BJ45 LOLed and OMGed over this episode intermittently for 3.24 hours.

When your boss calls you into his office to tell you that he has 'serious concerns' regarding your number of 'behavioural corrections', which has undergone a gradual yet substantial decline in recent months, your heart beats so fast the zing of metal fills your mouth. 'I'm sorry,' you say. 'I'll try harder.' 'That's what I like to hear,' says your boss. 'Because if you don't, we're going to be asking serious questions about your impact on company ethos.' Aside from that one time in Year 7 when your Geography teacher gave you a detention for not attempting to draw the earth 'by only the erroneous judgement of your own infantile eye', you have never been told off. As soon as he lets you go, you run to the bathroom mirror, open your mouth, and see that the blood isn't from your heart, but from your cheek, which you've chewed.

You need this job and yet you are incapable of trying. Now, when you spot Unproductive behaviour, you don't just do nothing, you zoom. Their screen is your screen and for a few intoxicating seconds, you are them.

User KL354
PlentyOfFish.Com

Looking For: I'll know when I see you, but whoever you are, you best not be a pussy, and I don't mean you've got to pull all that macho BS — I've met more than enough macho pussies to last a lifetime, TRUST ME — I mean you've got to have the guts to look me in the eye.

Interests: RnB & Come Dine With Me & Life &...

'Does this look like productive behaviour to you?' Your boss's chin brushes the crown of your head.

'Everyone, everyone, stop what you're doing and gather round!'

There's a chorus of chair twisting as everyone leaps away from their Mega Screens. The last time this many people looked at you was when you played the Third Donkey in the nativity play in primary school, and wet yourself. Your boss is talking, talking and talking and pointing, and you're surrounded by disapproving noises, but you don't really care because mostly, you're relieved not to be wetting yourself.

'Actually,' you say. 'I think it does. I think it's the most productive behaviour of all.' And even though it is only 3:23 p.m., you step into the stunned silence and you keep stepping until you can't see The Company's logo, or any screens, or MegaScreens, or Meeting Rooms or Secured Doors or ergonomic chairs, you're in some sort of post-industrial wilderness now, you've just passed a Costco and in the distance you see the blue and yellow blob of Ikea, but you keep going, further and further away from that office, hoping that one day you will meet User KL354, and that on this day there will be no screens between you, and you will tell each other and only each other exactly how it is.

Thirteen months before her death, seven months before her diagnosis, my wife grew afraid of sleep; she could no longer, she claimed, fall into it in our bed, but only on the living room sofa, in front of her favourite TV series, which, unfortunately for me, was *The Vicar of Dibley*.

I hated *The Vicar of Dibley*. She knew that I hated *The Vicar of Dibley*. For the years and the decades in which definitive endings only related to the lives of people who weren't us, she didn't bat an eyelid when, on hearing 'The Lord is my Shepherd', I would nip into the study and watch *Only Fools and Horses*.

But when the doctor confirmed what she, I now realise, already knew, I sacrificed my own personal tastes and watched it with her. I even managed to laugh at those repetitive wind-up-toy characters; Mr N-n-n-no-no and the endlessly stupid Alice and Hugo and that farmer chappy with the kind of beard which probably has food stuck in it on closer inspection. Me, laughing, at this nonsense! I turned to my wife, hoping she had noted my capacity for personal growth, even at this ripe old age. Lo and behold, she was asleep! Judging by the substantial puddle of drool on her collar, she had been for some time. Quite some time indeed.

'Why do you insist I watch that dire programme with you when you fall asleep as soon as it starts?' I complained the next morning.

She looked, for the second time in our fifty-two-year-long marriage, embarrassed. (The first was on our second date, when I had been talking at some length about Antarctica and she, having nodded and smiled and even asked a few pertinent-seeming questions, had asked whether the Antarcticans kept kangaroos as pets.) 'But if you weren't there,' she said, 'I wouldn't be able to fall asleep.'

'Why on earth not? You're tired all the damn time.'

Now, I can only kick myself for not being kinder in what I can no longer deny were the last months of her life. Then, I could only deny. Though as the months wore on, the end grew undeniable; she slept in the morning, the afternoon, the evening, the night. She woke up at lunchtime, at midnight, at five in the aft, at five in the morn. She only got out of bed when I lifted her, although it did not feel as if I was lifting my wife, so much as a strange bald bird who I loved and who still insisted on watching *The Vicar of Dibley* whenever she was awake enough to notice I was drawing the curtains. She would lean that bald bird's head against my chest and I would press my hand against her arm and we would lie there, neither asleep nor awake, needing nothing, not even to fight, for even now, at what I now saw was not so much a sudden event as the end of a process which had been happening, slowly, our entire lives, we were discovering a new and calm part of ourselves which had remained in the dark these fifty- two years.

No one else ever knew this part of my wife, not as I did, not with her bald head nodding to Mr N-n-n-n-no-no-no-no at *The Vicar of Dibley*; not even my children, who believe they know everything and that I, I am too doddery to notice how they always leave my house with bags that are a lot bigger and lumpier than the flat, empty things they arrived with, for they know me so little that they believe, also, I care whether I die with a house full of nick-nacks or a house only three-quarters full. No doubt they would hound me if they knew what I was keeping from them, but so be it; my wife spread herself out with so many people, it is only fair I have this to keep me warm, as *The Vicar* lulls me to sleep even though the rest of the woman without whom I would never be watching it is so annoyingly far away.

the impossibility of later

He said he would do the washing up later — as soon as he'd finished this chapter. Having done the washing up, he would clean the cooker. After that, his share of the housework would be on hiatus, he said, until his Magnum Opus was well and truly finished. 'Then,' he said, 'the flat will be my oyster; I will *even* clean under the fridge.'

'Yeah right,' said his partner. 'Just like how I was going to hoover under the bed last week. Let's face it, we're both too lazy to clean the places no one sees.'

'We're not lazy! We work hard. Listen, I will chain myself to this chair if needs be,' he said. 'Although, I might need your assistance so as to urinate and —'

'Whatever. Neither of us knows where to buy chains, let alone how to use them.'

'*That*,' he said, 'is plainly ridiculous.' Then he swivelled back to his screen, putting on his don't-interrupt-my-Magnum-Opus-with-your-idle-chit-chat face, even though the distinctive ping of his phone indicated to his partner and anyone else who might care about such things, that he'd just uploaded some photos from the recentish past onto Facebook.

not quite enough

He always keeps the light on longer than me and even though the light he keeps on is on his side of the bed and only spreads to my side as a dim glow, it robs me of anything from 20 to 60 minutes of sleep a night.

This may not sound like much in the Grand Scheme of Things, but it averages out as a deficit of 16425 minutes a year, and we have been married for seventeen and a half years, although it was only after the first child that I started to turn the light out before him, and that child is now a long-faced thirteen, so that makes 213525 minutes sleep which I will never, ever ever, not matter how long I live, get back; when you look at it like this, it looks, well, a *bit* grand. Don't you think?

Besides, if a Grand Scheme does exist, no one has ever shown it to me; life as I know it is made up of things small enough to cup in your hands — like flexible chrome lamps from Habitat (I am done with Ikea, *done!*).

I told all this to my friend, let's call her Becky. Becky is annoyingly practical. 'There's an obvious solution,' she said. 'Right here. Look.' She pointed to the Innovations catalogue, which she had dumped on my lap some time ago, but which I had been studiously ignoring because, to be honest, I was a bit embarrassed to be friends with someone who actually subscribed to a magazine of useless gadgets. Then I read the words: *clip-on reading lamp. Perfect for couples*. There was a blurred picture of a middle-aged couple; he was reading, she was sleeping; they could have been us. I closed the magazine. I felt a bit sick.

I told my friend I'd buy one later but she rolled her eyes. 'Later, like how you're always going to take up French or watercolours? That kind of later? Nothing ever happens in that kind of later. Do it now.' And then she dialled the 0800 number and thrust the phone into my hands.

After several long minutes of muzak, a human voice said hello. When I requested the clip-on reading lamp, I was greeted by a silence, then several clicks, then a sigh. 'Those are sold out. Very popular, I'm afraid. We should have some in about two weeks.'

I hung up without ordering. All over the country there were couples with the same problem as us — all of whom had solved this problem in the exact same way. Well I didn't want to be the same as them. I wanted to be us. I couldn't imagine waking up in the morning, groggy from not having had quite enough, and not having someone to blame.

midday in my mind

It's midday in my mind and it's waaay too bright. It's wowowowowowowow oh ha.

It's you and it's me and it's every speck of dust that dances between the molecules of air we can imagine (but never see) between us.

It's your legs. It's that scab on your left ankle which will never ever heal because you're forever colliding with the world's roughest edge.

It's that book I've been wanting to read but don't because I'm pretending to read the book you want me to read whilst actually reading the *Metro* and random links that people I've randomly followed on Twitter post to my home feed (although what kind of home this is or how it feeds me is a question I don't want to ask, let alone answer).

It's the sun lighting up the fuzz on your arms.

It's the buzz of your phone in your pocket and the way you thrust it out of the pocket and up into your face, as if it's so much more important than you and me, and all this everything this now this here this what do you call it this life?

'What was that?' you say, slipping your phone back into your pocket. 'It didn't really make sense.'

Your pocket. My eyes are glued to your pocket like a parched tongue to an open tap.

'Who was that,' I ask, pointing at the phone-shaped lump in your pocket.

'Oh.' You shrug. 'Just my brother. He's coming at 5.35 instead of 5.25 — you know how he likes to be exact.'

I don't say anything for a few seconds and then you wipe your pocket, even though it's perfectly clean. 'What, you don't like these jeans? What's wrong with you? Why were you saying so much so fast at once and now you won't speak?'

I breathe in deeply. I close my eyes, but it's no use; I need some hi-tech type of sunglasses — ones you can wear under your skin. 'It's not the jeans. It's the pocket. It looks so lovely and dark in there. I want to climb into it. I want to be where your phone is.'

Without opening my eyes to see your reaction, I reveal my final genius: 'It's taken me many years of field-based research to reach this conclusion, but... I've found the answer to modern life — the way to be everywhere at once. Everything would be much easier, for you, for me, for us, if I just turned into your phone.'

how the light gets out

repeat

I can see you staring at me. Yeah, you. You, in the mental socks. You with the hat. You with the hands that won't keep still.

And there's no need to look like that — like you wish you could disappear. You ain't the first one to stare and you won't be the last, that's for sure. Not every day you see a scar like this, eh? Big wet whopper of a curve cutting clean across my cheek. I'd fucking stare, if I was you. I'd think, how the hell does a young girl end up like that and to be honest almost every time I look in the mirror I ask myself the same question. How the hell did you end up like this? And then the question echoes back and forth, back and forth, like I'm me and someone else, or like I'm floating between the two, not sure which one to be.

Other times I just come out with it: yeah, yeah, I was in the Russian Mafia. I was kidnapped by guerillas on my gap yaarrr. Though no one believed any of that except this old biddy who ate her own lips, you know, the way old biddies do, and said, GORILLAS? YOU WERE KIDNAPPED BY GORILLAS?

Now I just say right off that yeah, yeah, as you're probably expecting, it happened when I was drunk. Pissed, hammered, blathered, laddered, sloshed, lashed, smashed, wasted, fucked. Also I was barefoot because way back in the light-dark-light-dark madness of the dance floor of the club my heel broke off and some girl tripped over it and starting having a go at me like I was the one controlling where she put her clumsy feet and so I stepped on her with my other heel and that one broke too and everything was thumping light-dark-light-dark-light-dark and everyone was dancing and the bouncers were grabbing my arms and lifting me up high over everyone and so I guess you could say they were the ones who decided I should leave. Yeah so all that was kind of sloshing around in my head and the less said about what was sloshing in (and out) of my belly the better and then this guy jumps out of the bushes that I didn't even notice were there until his hands were around my neck and so instead of thinking oh my fuck is he gonna kill me, I was all like, oh look at that bush it is full of buds.

His hands slide into my pockets, my pants, my bra. He's got one of those things like he's lost too much and he's worked himself up to thinking this is the time to get them all back. Fear flashed in his eyes and then I saw another flash: a knife.

And then this weird thing happened. So. Fucking. Weird. In scientific time it must have been half a second but in me-time it lasted long enough for me to see everything. I saw a beetle skidding across the pavement between our legs. I saw the throbbing of the warehouse where the people who were meant to be my mates were still raving — the lights flashing up the sky. I saw that I may well not live to be an old biddy. Didn't really feel anything when he did it; just saw his face get in a tangle with itself and then he ran off. When I got back to my flat, all I felt was wet. My housemate fainted when she saw me; when she woke up, she told me I was soaked in my own blood. I looked down at my top: last night it had been mustard yellow; now it was brown. 'Oh yeah.' But I still didn't feel any pain.

Now I just feel tangled; my mates are sick of this story, jammed on repeat, hoping that each telling will nudge me closer and closer to the end — to when I feel the cut of the blade.

is this it

The thing about the dark is... Anything could happen. A psycho could suffocate you with a Lidl bag, or a £50 note could blow into your face, or you could step on a slug.

Admittedly, a slug is more likely than a psycho, but it would still be traumatic, in its own slimy way, especially if you were wearing those nice silk socks your elderly aunt posted you for your birthday one month that was five months away from your actual birthday. Once you've peeled the socks off your feet, washed your feet (including your toes and all the gaps between them) and googled 'slug slime on silk socks — how to remove', it occurs to you that these socks and this aunt who doesn't quite know who you are, are both gifts from the dark.

Not that this actually happens. When your actual birthday comes around, when your flat is flashy with cameras and candles, when people you care for hand you lumps of paper which contain the physical proof of how much they know you, you cry. What's wrong? Why are you being such a baby? They say. Have you had too much champagne? She's had too much champagne. You've had too much champagne. Here, have some coffee in this new espresso pot I bought you. You're all grown up now. They say. Just look at all these candles. Now take a big breath. One, two, three and blow them all out!

You wipe away your tears and shut your eyes and blow out the candles. Then you down some more champagne (even though it's going flat). You are surrounded by wrapping paper, by kind words and kinder faces, by things you have asked for and even, in the case of the massage tokens, dreamt about. But you can't help wondering whether this really is it. Is this everything? All you want to do is to sit in the dark and stroke the silk sock that was meant for a person you never quite got to be.

have you seen this person?

Do these badly printed pixels mean anything to you?

You have the right to remain silent but any failure to cooperate may be used as evidence against you or against this person you, in your stubborn silence, are indicating you've never seen.

You have the right to remain silent but we have strong reason to suspect that when faced with the facts, you will change your mind.

Exhibit One: the hood. Or more precisely: its shadow. Yes, the hood and its shadow must mean something to this person because this person has never been seen without it, not even when the summer heat puts forces in this county and even in the next county along on high alert for riots.

Exhibit Two: greed. This person wants more than they already have, and they are willing to break the law in order to feel its weight in their palms, They are willing to steal a Spaghetti Hoops 4-pack (07/06/2012 — Heron Foods CCTV), Colgate milk teeth x 3 (09/10/2013 — Pound Stretcher CCTV), chocolate Santa stocking pack, (23/12/2013 — 99p Store CCTV).

We also have strong reason to suspect they are willing to smash the window of JD Sports with a (stolen) parasol stick, climb in, then climb out with as many pairs of bright white trainers as their puny arms can carry. (CCTV footage for this infraction cannot be located; however, one member of the public who, rather than allowing himself to be dragged down by the rioters, stood back and captured the criminal activity so as to strengthen Law and Order in Boshcombe and County going forward.)

Exhibit Three: the *Boshcombe News*, pp.14−15. A badly pixelated version of this person has appeared in this newspaper almost every week for 1.8 years. A person who was not the person we are looking for rang in to say that they had seen a person who looked like the badly pixelated person carefully cutting out the photo of the badly pixelated person then — with a suspicious degree of care — slipping it into a plastic wallet. The person who was not the person we are looking for claimed all this happened in Caffé Nero. We have not pursued this claim; we have watched the person we are looking for for 2.15 years now, and we have strong reason to believe they would never frequent Caffé Nero.

Exhibit Five: your smirk. Yes, we have seen how you smirk when you thumb to pp.14−15 of the *Boshcombe News* each Friday. You have the right to remain silent and we'd suggest this is what you do. We'd suggest you use your silence to get your story straight by the time we reach the station. You see, we've been doing this long enough to sniff out every last drop of guilt within county boundaries (go over the border, and there is nothing we can do; you'll have to refer yourself to the authorities there). Yes, you know this person alright. You know those fingers that won't stop moving until they've found what you want. You know how it is to be out at twilight and to duck and swerve away from dark threatening shapes that don't, after all, exist beyond the boundaries of your own body. You know how strange this body can feel and sometimes, sometimes, you stare at its surface until its meaning blurs and it's almost as if it is made up of pixels so crude they will never quite make a whole.

this application will save your life

You know that thing you've been missing — the thing you don't even know is missing until its absence punches a clean white hole in your blank duvet of sleep? Well… it's me.

Oh, I know! It'll take a minute to sink in, maybe two. Or even three.

Not to blow my own trumpet or anything — although I'll just add that it is an incredibly shiny trumpet — but my most recent role was Third Woman with Sore Head in ITV's new hospital drama, *A&E Hearts*. In the words of the critics, I was 'the most convincing Third Woman with Sore Head' ever to grace ITV's screen.

These critics, I should add, were my friends. Also my sister and her cat and her rabbit (although between you and me, I'm not sure rabbits have the critical powers to tell a bad carrot from a good one, let alone develop a point of view on art). Anyway, these critics can be harsh! In one of my early roles, for example — Girl with Consumption 2 in *Pale Ladies — Pilot* — they insisted that I looked far too rosy-cheeked and pleased with myself to have consumption. So when they said I'd got Third Woman With Sore Head spot on, they meant it; even though, they said, I was in the corner of the screen, even though the script left no room to explore the origins of my pain, the depth of the crease on my forehead was such that their eyes were drawn from the main action; it was clearly a very bad, very deep, very very terrible pain indeed.

So if there's anyone who is destined to be the face of Accident and Emergency Insurance Cover; if there's anyone who can convince the viewers of Living (daytime) TV that they can avoid life's potholes and slippery slopes with one small monthly payment, it's me.

a shock

Everyone was shocked when he threw himself off the tower of that church only a quarter of a mile from the college where he was Secretary of the Boat Club, JCR Social Secretary, a member of the Ball Committee and the Charitable Committee, and, according to both his Philosophy and Politics tutors, one of the most academically gifted students they had met in recent years. To the eulogies given by the Chairs and Vice Secretaries of these various clubs and societies of which he had been such an integral — not to mention 'banterous' part — his family added only that from birth, he had been the favourite. But no one was as shocked as the woman who, at the moment at which he made the last decision he was ever going to make, was eating a cake in the church cafe garden, a few hundred metres below and — fortunately — several metres to the left of him. The cake was gluten free.

daylight robbery

He grabs my collar and says, 'You're not going to get away with it.'

'Get away with what?' I reply. 'Chatting to the boy in the kebab shop?'

'You weren't chatting,' he says, spitting his t's all over my cheeks. 'You were *flirting*. You would've gone behind the counter and wanked him off if I hadn't come in.'

'We were talking,' I say, 'about the weather. It's a beautiful day, don't you think?'

He lets me go, puts his hands on his hips and turns around. His chest grows and shrinks inside his T-shirt — massive one minute, teeny the next, depending on how much air there is in his lungs.

We both face the water and the trees, and the reflection of the trees swimming about in the water, and I hope he feels the sun on his back the way I do — how kind it is. Bike bells clang, kids scream; on a street not too far from this canal, 'Oranges and Lemons' jangles from an ice cream van. I would quite like an ice cream. I would quite like to see my kids again, to be a kid again; I would like to enjoy the sun without this tightness in my belly asking, what's he going to do next? He won't do anything, I tell it. He's looking at the water. And we keep having to move out of the way for runners, cyclists, walkers, puffy-eyed young couples with prams.

'Thought that was it, didn't you?' his face is in my face. His breath is where my breath should be. His hands are on my neck his fingers are where the air should be there is a woman jogging past with pretty pink headphones jammed into her ears I want to scream I want to shout I want someone to turn and look what is happening to me I want to see the horror in someone else's eyes because it's broad daylight it's high summer it's ice cream time it's advert time and I can't really believe it

I can't even
See it
All I see is
Is is
This is
The daylight robbery

dark places to watch out for [4]

Gravity. The bastard. Cracking the hips of old people. Skinning the knees of the young. And periodically pulling at the faces of all those in the middle, reminding them that they will not stay in the middle forever; encouraging them to fork out for creams which claim to fight off gravity with more *umph* than would nature.

The desire to laugh in what everyone agrees is a Very Important Meeting and which, the more you remind yourself How Important This Is, only grows to a cough that even thoughts of massacres and holocausts and the death of your family and the nuclear apocalypse cannot suppress.

The tiny holes in the concrete which is meant to fill the cracks between paving stones; millions of ants live there.

Those mornings when the prospect of the day is like a morbidly obese man sitting on your stomach, stubbornly refusing to let you get up and get on with your life.

The voice that whines, Why? Why why why why why why why? Especially when you cross the street to avoid a charity mugger only to bump into a mugger from a different charity, one which dresses its agents in purple T-shirts rather than red ones.

The darkness in the belly of a can of Diet Coke, crushed, which you find on an otherwise pristine moor.

No matter how many times you tell everyone — in person, on the phone, in person again, on Facebook, on Twitter, on Instagram, on Facebook again and again — that you are having a brilliant time, this time is not brilliant and you do not feel, in your heart of darkest hearts, that you are having it, but rather, that it is having you.

not talking about it

You didn't want to talk about it, you just wanted to be normal, is the first thing you said to me, even before you said hello.

'That's good,' I replied, 'because being normal is something I still don't know how to do.'

You looked at me like I was a bit mental. 'Oh you know,' you said, 'like just shop and have fun.'

What you didn't and still don't know about me is, shopping, particularly clothes shopping, is the closest thing I've experienced to HELL. But you had just lived through darknesses I could only — and didn't particularly want to — imagine, this was one of your first attempts to scoop up the frayed remains of your previous life, so who was I to stop you?

So we went shopping. And I don't know if you noticed, but with that thing we weren't allowed to talk about following us around, it was worse. It was worse than hell. Imagine a tantrum-filled toddler stomping at your side as you examine Topshop's latest collection of play suits. Imagine it screaming, tugging at your skirt, biting your ankle. Imagine that no one can see or it it but you and me, and the more we ignore it, the louder it screams.

From Topshop to New Look to American Apparel to Primark to H&M and finally to Zara, where it hit the gravelly bottom of that imaginary toddler tantrum underworld. I, lacking the energy to take off my coat and my shoes and my clothes only to have my body so uncompromisingly revealed to me in those over-bright three-way mirrors, was slumped on a plastic chair outside your cubicle, placed there by some kind soul — thank you! thank you! — for weirdos exactly like me. You pulled back the cubicle curtain, stepped towards me and twirled.

'What do you think? Does it make it look a bit... You know?'

'Umm...' It was hard for me to reply, given that the toddler was yanking the tassels which dangled from the hem of your lemon sorbet coloured dress, whilst making a noise far more hideous than any toddler would make in not-only-imaginary life. The toddler wanted to strip you of this dress; to wrestle you to the floor until you threw your arms around its pudgy shoulders and, at long last, paid it some attention.

You twirl again. 'Do you like it? It's just, I can kind of imagine having a fun night in it, which is kinda cool given that, you know, like last week or the week before, I swore to myself I'd never have fun, like, ever ever again...'

I waited for you to do something about the toddler but instead you raised one eyebrow and crossed your arms and sighed, just like you used to, back before the thing we were not talking about, when you were giving me one more chance to ward off your wrath.

'It's lovely,' I said, even though it flapped and clung in all the wrong places and made you look jaundiced. 'It's just right.'

You smiled and clapped your hands and got changed and queued up and filled out a form for the Zara reward card and, just when I had resigned myself to spending the rest of my life in that shop, with Rihanna playing on a loop, you waved a large paper bag in my face and dragged me out into the street.

The street, although lined with shops and people desperate to get into shops, was not a shop; for this I was glad. When I looked down, the toddler had climbed into your bag and was nesting in the gauzy layers of your dress. Its eyelids were drooping, as if it needed to sleep but wasn't ready to let the world go just yet.

'This was fun,' you said, yawning.

Fun? I don't think so. But I wanted it to be as much as you did, and if this, I thought, watching the toddler finally nod off, was the only way I could help rebuild your world as a fun one, I would. And so I said yes. I said, yes, this was really fun. You looked so happy when I said this, that I added, 'Let's do it again soon.' 'Yes, let's!' you said, and then you walked off, the dress and the imaginary toddler swinging from your left arm, and I didn't even feel too bleak although it was obvious we were going to have to live with this toddler for the foreseeable, I had a feeling that the next time we took it out, it would be, if not on its best behaviour, a little more placid.

happy, sad, numb

Don't look, Mum tells us. *Keep your hat on, your head down. Why don't you imagine a cute fluffy rabbit nibbling crumbs people have carelessly dropped on the floor?* The problem is, we imagine the rabbits so clearly that the smelly woman behind us tells us to hurry the fuck up and then Mum turns around and tells her to mind your language thank you very much and the smelly woman laughs and laughs and then pushes us out of the queue.

Teachers tell us the hungry people are in Africa. They are brown and they live in huts. Flies always buzz around their eyes. *There is hunger in this country too*, we tell her. She shakes her head as if we are silly little children. Oh, but it's not the same, she says. We narrow our eyes at her. We may be children and we may be the joint second littlest in the class, but we know what it is to climb into bed with the emptiness in your belly filling your head with cream cakes and bacon and roast potatoes and pizza and a million other things you'll never get, at least, not from the huge metal pots at the Food Bank.

Sandrine Willis tells us we are tramps. Between her and us we stuff the memory of her mum shouting at her to *shove the food tokens in the bin they are for tramps we're not tramps*; it softens her words, but only a bit.

Another thing Mum tells us is that soon, things will get better. Soon, we will eat dinner at home every night (and home will feel like a home because the bailiffs will give back our sofas and the electric will always be on and there will be money for the heaters). *But it's better to start now*, she says, the night we sit next to the woman who wipes her nose with her bread. *It's better to already start forgetting you were ever here.* And so we stare at the plastic tablecloths. We stare at the three round cushions in the children's corner with the faces on: happy, sad, numb. We try to forget. But we can't. We can't.

You see, this place, this space, it is in us. Our arteries stiffen like the bare beige walls whenever someone (anyone) stares at the stains on our coats a little too long. Stamping our feet on the paving stones, waiting for the doors to open up, then waiting again to reach the food, waiting to see what will come out of the pot, waiting to see which table we will get and who will be next to us, cutting our food into tinier and tinier pieces so that when our plates are empty we will feel sure this is enough, wondering, as we sneak back into the outside, is anyone going to see us; each bit lasts a few minutes, but over days, weeks, months, it adds up; the *soon* our Mum keeps telling us about is still not here to get us, and people, they can see this *now* that we are in flashing across our eyes, beating creases into our foreheads that are deep and dark: we don't blame them for being scared of us.

And when some teacher (or other adult whose full belly

won't let them sleep at night until they've at least tried to be kind) finally stops and asks, how are we feeling? Are we all right? All we will see are those three round cushions: happy, sad, numb.

You won't see me, not even if you look. Although most of the time, you don't, do you? Most of the time, you are hunched over your iPhone. Most of the time, your feet are on the pavement whilst your mind is already wrapped up warm in your boyfriend's arms, on your newish Ikea sofa, in your newish flat way up on the tenth floor.

From where I am, your life is a rectangle of golden light — the exact size, shape and colour of one of those budget cough sweets which do absolutely nothing to get rid of your cough. Your ankles are the part of you I know best: they are dry and pointy and often purple with scabs.

Some nights, as the sun is going down and I know it's a matter of minutes before the shivering sets in, I imagine my life from where you are. I imagine I'm you, leaning over the balcony, arms on the railings, feet by the barbeque you're not meant to have in your building (it's alright, I won't tell anyone); the sunset throws the derelict factories, the railway tracks and even the empty car parks into a glamorous light; you rush for your iPhone, click-click-click, but it's no use; the lens can't capture the play of light against the time-nibbled brick. Your photo is all shadowy lumps which leave a sour taste in your mouth. Nope, this is just a sunset, not a

#sunset. No one else will know about it. And you're glad. You turn your back on the city, and for once you're grateful for all that awaits on the inside of your balcony doors: powdered hot chocolate, a microwave, a boyfriend with whom you can almost comfortably share your small, ripped sofa, and Netflix.

the other lady of the night

When they said I'd become a lady of the night, I saw funfairs. I looked into the black-black of the container and I saw the Big Wheel spin me up, spin me down, spin me round and round.

There were a lot of other English words in my head; I told the other girls what they meant; they joked that my brain was the size of two fat chickens, but I didn't want to think about chickens and how hard my body longed to eat them, so I told them how 'lady' also meant rich woman, 'girl' meant child as well as woman and 'bird' meant not only a bird but a woman who did nothing but fuck.

Will we be friends with the Queen? the other girls asked. Not *friends*, I said, but maybe we'll bump into her at a party. Maybe she'll do her extra special wave — like this! I mimed the wave to the girls, they laughed so hard their shoulders knocked against one another, and for a moment, I forgot where we were, what we were soon going to be; we hadn't seen natural light, a shower, or real food for days, and yet for those few seconds, I felt something like loved. And this extra special wave, I said, it won't be for anyone; it will be just for us.

But when their laughter died away, when the sea was

rocking and there was nowhere to go but the lonely vacuum of sleep, I closed my eyes and saw fireworks. I saw sparks ripping open the sky on my parents' TV last New Year's Eve; I saw them down Special Christmas Vodka, I was only thirteen and trying to sip Special Christmas Vodka without them knowing, and all over the TV there were sparks, everyone was cheering and clapping, even my parents were cheering and clapping, except I was forgetting to cheer and clap because I was already trying to work out how I'd get to England and become this spark that the whole world would cheer from the TV. Yes, sparks were what we were making this long black journey to be.

I only questioned what a Lady of the Night might be when Passport spat it through the gap where his tooth was meant to be. He stared at us until we squirmed; then, a mean muddy snort fell from his nostrils. The other girls cried like babies. I ignored him. Passport didn't scare me. I'd seen him kiss the girlfriend in his phone. I'd seen him pick his nose. I knew his real name wasn't Passport; he only made us call him it so we'd feel scared and he'd feel big but if I stood up next to him, I could look down on the shiny skin of his head where his hair had forgotten to grow.

I don't even know where the other girls are now. For a long, long time I didn't know where I was; all I knew was the darkness and the cold and the eyes of the people who smile when they spit at us in the street — people so poor they have broken skin and broken faces and Cornflake packets covering the breaks in their windows and not even any goats — because who else are they allowed to hate if not us?

One man told me we were in Wakefield. His cock was in my mouth and I thought, maybe my brain has finally melted and these words are coming from this cock, but then my mouth filled with hot salty slime and I sat up and I swallowed and I saw that the words is coming from his mouth not his cock.

'So, what do you reckon to Wakefield then?' said his mouth. *Wakefield*? It's not even a famous town — never on the TV back home.

'Is Wakefield city?' I asked.

He laughed and looked at me like I was the idiot no.1 of the village. 'No way. If it's a city you're after, get yourself along to Leeds.'

When I didn't say anything back he slapped me and said of course you don't understand a thing, do you, you dirty Polish bitch. I've never been to Poland, but there was no time to say this before he kicked me out of the car.

Kicking Ladies out of the car is not in the Rules. The Rules say he paid extra to drive me out so long as he drove right back. In the Rules we knew but which he'd never know until it was too late, they'd beat him up if he didn't bring me back; then they'd find me and beat me up too and maybe my life would end right there under their fists or maybe it would go on a bit; the Rules didn't say any of this; this I knew from the rules too strong to put into words.

The car sped off and so did Mr Wakefield and so I stood, pulled on the tights I kept in my bag just in case, and walked. It was dark, very dark; there were no street lights, no houses, no Londis, no William Hill or KFC. Just trees and grass and hedge and gravel and some dark round shapes I convinced myself were some soft round living thing, like sheep. Yes, sheep. I folded back my head and looked up at the sky. This was the first time I'd seen the stars since I waved goodbye to my parents and their TV.

I walked and I walked until I saw a yellow square of light. It was a very small square, very far away, but I walked towards it. I walked over grass and stepped in many cow shits but I didn't even care. I fixed my eye on the light until it grew to fill me. I didn't know what I'd find there, but hope sparked all over my body; it sparked like the fireworks in London. Maybe at last I would meet her, the Lady of the Night I imagined at the start of this story; maybe I'd give her a big hug and refuse let go until we were both set free.

learning to live with cracks again

dark places to watch out for [5]

No matter the tongue-in-cheek and cheek-in-tongue self-help books; no matter the Om-free yoga classes, the quality dinners with quality friends, the hand-roasted fair trade organic coffee; no matter the tantric sex; no matter the early nights and wholegrain pasta; no matter the black belt in karate and the cabinet of medals, certificates and rare vinyls; no matter if you can illuminate the world's capital cities with your own personal light bulb moments; when that phone rings, when you trip, fall or slowly, slowly slide back into that dark place, it will not feel like any darkness you've known before. It will suck. And digging your way out will not be any easier than it was the last time, or the time before, and the people who offer you pitying I-know-how-it-is glances and say shit like, 'This book I read has just the answer: the route out is always one no one has ever mapped before' — you will hate them no less.

how to talk about potholes

Our father collects potholes.

He photographs them.

Squats down in the middle of the road — in a HighVis vest he purchased from, as he put it a, 'manual labour chappy's' shop — and measures their circumference, diameter and depth. He pulls out his compass and works out their three-figure bearing. We have tried and tried to explain about GPS but he is 'not having some piddling phone telling me what's what, thank you very much!' He collects this information in an Excel spreadsheet which he has printed out — large scale — and fastened to a clipboard which he keeps in the passenger seat of his car, which is, as the sympathetic middle middle child among us pointed out, exactly where our mother used to sit.

Back at home, our father copies his findings into a digital spreadsheet. Every Friday, he prints out and posts the most up-to-date version to the council. Every month, they reply with the same letter which thanks him for getting in touch and says that if he wants a more immediate response he should contact them by email, or, if his issue is really urgent, via their new live chat facility. The sympathetic middle middle child had to explain to him that a new live chat facility meant typing a question into a window on the computer screen then waiting for someone to type back.

'That's outrageous,' he said. 'What do they think I am, some kind of IMBECILE?' He then went on to berate the sympathetic middle middle child for treating him like one. We told the sympathetic middle middle child that she did not have to take this; she did not have to look after him. But she shrugged and made a face which reminded us that she felt like she owed him for the time he took her in when her marriage caved in on itself; we do not push the matter further as we are well aware that we were too caught up in our own lives to help her out at this difficult time; this is a lack of which we are far from proud.

Whenever we ring our father to ask how he is feeling — or, feeling particularly generous or guilty, or remembering there is an item of furniture we want to nab from the house before the others do and we drop in — he will talk only about potholes. 'Just this morning, I found one packed to the brim with the excrement of at least three different kinds of mammals!' We don't care about potholes and we definitely don't care about which or how many kinds of excrement he has found inside of them. But we do care about our dad and we want to know: does he eat? Does he sleep? Does he feel a part of human life? Does he have hopes and plans for the future? But he will only reply by treating us to a slide show of that week's most unusual potholes.

Only the sympathetic middle middle child dared ask him

outright: 'Daddy, do you think you're trying to replace Mum with these, these potholes?'

For the first time since the start of this whole pothole thing, Dad was silent. Then he spoke: 'Quite the opposite. I've been wanting to make a proper inventory of our area's potholes for years. But your mum always stopped me — oh, you're enough of a crank as it is, oh, so-and-so and so-and-so are coming for lunch so you won't have time, etc., etc. But now I don't have to invite any sos over for lunch. I don't have to care if I'm too much of a crank! I can do what I want!'

For the first time since forever, all four of us were silent. And for the first time since her death nine months ago, we collectively 'got' the loss of our mother; our purpose was to mock our father, her purpose was to tell us off for mocking him then persuade him out of his more hideously mockable qualities using more subtle, manipulative means. But she was not here any more and her not being here means that we would have to learn to be here in a whole new way.

'Dad,' said another of us, the second eldest / eldest middle child and a freelance web some-thing-or-other of whom the rest of us have always been a little afraid. 'Why don't you get this stuff out to an audience? Like, people who actually care. Because there are a lot of people who care about potholes but not the council. At least, not as much as you.'

And so the seeds of potholesofwestyorkshire.co.uk were sown. It gets up to 10,000 hits a week, or so the eldest middle child tells us. Our father has a certain fame amongst the region's pothole cranks and has even been asked to speak at some pothole conference. Now, when we see him, he talks a little less about potholes, and although we are relieved, and are sure this is some sign of progress, we are not sure what this sign means, or what, if anything, we will talk to our father about instead.

the moon on your face

It was my friend's kid what did it. I had gone round to see my friend but then she'd 'popped to the shops', leaving me with her kid, which I wasn't too happy about seeing as her kid was a proper brat. At least, that's what I thought. I was sitting on my friend's sagging sofa, waiting for the kid's proper brattish nature to come out.

But the kid just stared at me. It stared and it stared and eventually I asked if it wanted a Choc Ice or something — my observation of other peoples' kids suggested almost every problem in life could be solved with a Choc Ice — but it shook its head — okay, it was a *he*, I guess I should stop calling it *it* — and said, 'It looks like the moon.'

It was a moment before I clocked that by 'it' he meant my scar. The next thing I clocked was that he'd been staring at it and I hadn't shouted at him or had to sit on my hands to stop from slapping him; my throat hadn't filled with tears; I hadn't even noticed, and now that I had, I didn't mind.

'I would like a slice of the moon on my face,' he said, edging towards me. 'You're lucky.'

I laughed, and was about to say that he wouldn't think I was lucky if he knew how I got it. But then the door slammed, and I could hear my friend stomping down the corridor, yelling at the kid that he better not have done anything bad, and I thought: maybe the kid is right. Maybe I am lucky. That scar, and the story of how I got it, and the part of my life that will be forever curled up in that story, is a slice of another world most people will only ever watch on the telly.

'What's up with you?' asked my friend. 'You look like you've seen a ghost.'

'Something like that,' I said, stroking my own personal slice of somewhere else.

discovery in the dark

There are things you can discover at that moment when you have been awake so long on your back on your bed, wriggling and squiggling through your partner's snores, when you have stared through the light and the dark and are now in some strange never-ending beyond. These things include the knowledge that you would take the time to pack your laptop and your laptop charger and your phone and your phone charger and your iPod and your iPod charger and your Kindle and your Kindle charger if, in this hypothetical anti-time-space into which you have inconveniently fallen, someone were to call you tomorrow and tell you that someone you love who is in a different country to you is about to die. You know this as clearly as you know that morning will never come, even though you also know that you know a few people in other countries but you do not love them.

why i'm not scared

I'm not scared of the dark, but my sisters are and so we have to sleep with the Night Light, which means *they* get to sleep and snore and dream and dribble whilst I'm like so awake I think I'll burst.

This is like so unfair but Mummy says it would be even more so unfair not to have the Night Light because there are two of them and one of me. I said it's not my fault they're twins and I'm not. She said, stop being mean and eat your dinner! Another thing she says is that the Night Light isn't very bright. Well why don't you get one in your room? I said. She said, eat your dinner. It's always, always, eat your dinner.

Sometimes, when I get bored of watching the twins' eyes flicker at the same time — they're like so so boring they can't even be bothered to come up with their own dreams — I go downstairs and stand on a chair and turn off the burglar alarm. Dad only puts on the alarm at night because burglars are afraid of the daylight, except I don't actually think that's true because the next thing I do after I've turned off the alarm is I creep out into the garden and there are no burglars — absolutely none at all.

There is sloshy, slimy grass. There are slugs. There are snails. There are slugs and snails I have accidentally murdered with my feet. There are stars and a bit of moon and sometimes, sometimes, music that thumps through the ground from that house down the road with the dirty windows and rubbishy garden that Mummy and Daddy don't like.

The darkest place of all is the gap between the shed and the wall; it's also my most favouritest place. I crouch and stare at the darkness until it's not even black but like dancing with so so so many colours that sometimes I'm not sure if I'm awake or asleep. I'm not sure if these colours are, like, stuck to the backs of my eyelids and all this darkness and its weird wiggling dancing colours are all inside me.

no further than a selfie stick

Your neck is licking distance from my tongue and has been for the past seven weeks, five days and 23 hours, and yet we're no closer to the bottom or even the middle of this endless muddy story than when our bodies were on opposite sides of this vast tilted world.

'Stop staring at me,' you mumble, without turning around.

'You're so fucking self-centred,' I say. 'I was actually asleep. I was actually dreaming about… About that woman we met on Blackfriars Bridge.'

Your downy neck hairs bristle. 'You mean the woman who took our photograph? What are you dreaming about *her* for? We don't even know her.'

'I'm pretty sure she thought we were siblings,' I say, then I stroke your neck and add, 'These hairs, they're the same as when we were kids.'

'Not this again.' You flop onto your side, and where your eyes should be, I see two worlds — vast, tilted, unknowable. You kiss me on the nose. 'We're here. Pissing each other off in the same bed. Isn't this all we've dreamed of, for years?' You roll onto the floor. 'Now let's do something fun. We're in one of the world's most popular cities, after all.'

I sit up. But something — perhaps it's the strange new light peeping round the edge of the drawing-pinned sheet that passes for a curtain, perhaps it's random, perhaps it's the moon — stops me from leaping into the comfortable groove of routine.

'But we've been to the museums. We've walked across the bridges, we've groaned at the street performers at Covent Garden, we've eaten free chunks of cheese at Borough Market. We've dodged hipster bikes on the Regent's Canal, we've drunk tea from china cups in ex-factories in Hackney Wick. We've been to *both* Westfields. We've — '

'Alexandra Palace! We haven't been there yet.' You stuff your legs into your jeans in the manner of a spy film baddie. 'Or Crystal Palace. I was just last night googling — '

'And each time,' I say, tucking the duvet around my bare limbs for protection, although against what, I've no idea, 'you grab some stranger, you tell them we're lost, or we need them to take a photo, and then you thrust them between us, into this gap, this, you know…' I flap at the air. 'All this!'

'Okay,' you say, raising your hands, again, in imitation of someone who's imitating something else. 'But have you seen how much damp there is on the ceiling? I can't discuss this properly, not with the damp on the ceiling.'

Three trains, two Mars bars and forty-three minutes later, and we're staring at the flaking skin of the Crystal Park dinosaurs. We're the only people looking at the dinosaurs;

the nearest bunch of kids are crowded around some kind of Nintendo.

'All that time we were living apart,' I begin, 'I had this ache in my side, like I was missing this precious thing. All we needed, I thought, was to be back in the same city, the same bed, and — '

'Look!' You yank me away from the rusted metal fence that protects the dinosaurs from all the people who're not interested in them. 'That dude.' The Nintendo kids are now hovering around a man whose hand dangles with long black things. 'He's selling selfie sticks.'

I'm too shocked to tell you how shocked I am that I'm sharing my life with someone who is genuinely excited by the prospect of a selfie stick. Something drips on my chest — not rain or bird poo or some Sign from God, but my own drool.

'We won't have to, as you put it, *stick strangers* between us any more. And we don't have to put up with their shitty photography skills, either. We can take photos of ourselves exactly as we want!'

I don't really care about photos, but I can't tell you this or anything else because you're already marching over to Mr Selfie Stick and the Nintendo kids.

'£12.99 for two!' you exclaim. 'Bargain, eh?'

I roll my eyes but my fingers are already slipping my phone into the stick's sleek plastic grip. Pressing the camera icon, I stretch out my arm until it's at the distance a stranger would be. At the tick, tick, tick of the timer you smash your lips against my cheek.

Then you grab the stick and hold my phone so close to your face, I can't see the version of us that you see. 'You look alright,' you say, 'but I look hideous. And you can't even see the dinosaurs. All you can see is that crappy fence. Let's try with mine — no, let's do both at the same time.'

I hold out my stick; you hold out yours. Tick, tick, tick and, snap! You throw your arm around my shoulder and I lean my head on yours and we smile.

I stare at my version of us; you stare at yours. What I see is a boy and a girl, alone in a house that is itself alone on a cliff that is itself alone. These two children build a world around each other — a world of sand and driftwood, shards of grass washed blunt by the sea, of rocks and the dark crabby cracks between. The prospect that the world might one day be wrenched from them is so terrifying, they promise one another that when they grow up, they'll get married — even though, being brother and sister, this is Not Allowed.

'Look.' You thrust your version on top of my version. Then you look me in the eye for the first time in these sevenish weeks. 'This reminds me of the day we found out. Remember?'

'Of course I remember.'

'How we look here — it's how we, how *I* felt, that day.'

I look at your version of us. Then my version. Your version, my version... All I see are two human beings, trying to work out what or where they are. The dinosaurs blur into the trees. They could be anywhere. They could be anyone.

'It was strange, because all those years I'd wished we weren't brother and sister so we could, you know… And then when "Mum" died and we found out we actually weren't, it was the scariest thing in the world. Because once your wishes come true, where do you go?'

'You run away to the other side of the world.' Because this is what you did: you bought a one way ticket in the opposite direction from our lie-riddled childhood.

Your cheeks shine with tears. 'I'm so sorry. But I'm here now. And so are you. Isn't that the point?'

Over your shoulder I notice that the Nintendo kids are staring, not at the dinosaurs, but at us. 'You're right,' I say. 'Today does feel like that day. Because, if there's no outside reason we can't be together, no blood ties, or air miles, who can we blame for all this, you know, this, this, *distance* between us?'

You point to the smiling faces on our phone screens. 'Between this us and that us? I blame life. I blame death. I blame our — your — parents. I blame exhaust fumes and GM crops and gluten. Most of all, I blame the selfie stick.'

I bite my lip to keep from laughing; I'm not ready to stop being pissed off with you yet. 'So why did you buy them then?'

As you stare at the shining plastic antennae, I spy in your little eye, sadness. And suddenly, for the first time in ages, maybe even since we were kids on that house on the cliff, I move with the conviction that the thing I'm about to do is the only and correct one: I grab the selfie stick.

'What the fuck? Let go!'

But I pull harder. So do you. I pinch your waist; you squeal, kick my shins. I howl.

Pretty soon we are rolling over in the grass, no way to discern the beginning, the ends or even the middle of you, me or either of the selfie sticks. I've missed this.

'Look! They're having sex!'

'That's not sex; it's fighting.'

The Ninetendo kids. The Ninetendo kids poke at the edges of my vision.

'Reckon we should stop them? You should stop that you know. You're going to break those sticks.'

'Or each other. Fights break people, you know.'

'Should we call the police?'

On the word 'police' you let go of my wrist; there's a stinging red ring where your fingers were. You look at me, look up at the kids, look back to me; it's as if you're seeing me for the first time. We roll away from each other, stand up and de-grass-and-mud our thighs and arses. The selfie sticks are a dark heap between us.

'You two made up now?' says one of the Ninetendo kids.

I stare at one of the dinosaur's nostrils to ensure I don't laugh. 'Maybe. Maybe.'

'Just don't pull that shit again, yeah? It's weird.'

'We won't,' you say, grabbing my arm. 'Trust me, we won't.'

'Don't you want those sticks?' shouts one of the Nintendo kids.

'Nah,' you say. 'We don't need them any more. They're yours if you want them.'

The Nintendo kids leap towards those dark shapes in the grass, their limbs alight with the belief that here, at last, is the precious shiny thing they're missing, the thing — and it's only now, at the grand old age of 26, that I'm able to admit this — is never so shiny or precious by the time it reaches your grubby palms.

'Should we talk about what just happened?'

'No.'

'Phew.'

You're stabbing your phone. 'I'd saved a *Time Out* page about twelve things you had to do in London this weekend, but there's no fucking 4G …'

'Ssshh.' I rub your back. I rub your back the way the woman who turned out to be my mum but not yours rubbed our backs when we grazed our knees or got sick or life otherwise failed to work out as we'd hoped. 'Let's just walk. Let's see where our feet take us.'

And we do. We walk until we don't know what or who or where we are, only that we're muddy and messy and precious.

do not alight here

I used to think that everyone's Mummy had a different life in a different place with a different name and a Daddy who tried so many times to kill her that they locked him up and threw away the key. I used to think everyone jumped at every creak and whistle in the night, thinking, What if that's *him*? What if he found the key? I used to think that the Daddies I saw at the school gates and in my friends' kitchens could not be the real Daddies, who were locked up, along with my Daddy, in the place of no keys.

But as I grew old enough to spend more time out of my Mum's house than in, I realised that for other people, this world was the only one. These Daddies who used to swing them on their shoulders and now taught them how to drive and gave them boring lectures on what to study at Uni, were their real ones. Their mistake was in thinking this was the only world, and the other world, the unmentionable swirl of darkness, a figment of their melodramatic teenage imaginations; and how terrifying it would be when sooner or later life dumped them in it, lacking as they did the muscles to leap back and forth across the borders I am now grateful I can see.

unnecessary attachments

You are deleting unnecessary attachments from your work inbox whilst trying not to listen to your boss's reenactment of what he has already memorialised, hilariously, as 'Scubagate', when the thought crosses your mind that you will die as a human who has never scuba-dived. No *probably*. Not even a *maybe*. Your bones know you will never scuba-dive in the same way that they know you will never fully relax around cats; will always wake up seven to nine minutes before your alarm, regardless of the time for which it is set; and more often than not, you will experience a dull ache in your heart whenever you hear the word 'party'. Yes, you will die without doing or being many things; you will die as you are — and perhaps that is alright.

You look up from your computer, in search of some human to share this lightbulb moment with. But all heads are crowded round the small luminous screen of your boss's phone, cooing as if he has just invented some new and better-than-human form of life.

'What is it?' you say, despite yourself.

'Pics from the underwater camera. Bloody expensive, but well worth it, don't you think?!' says your boss as he waves the phone in your face. On the screen, smudged by greasy, eager thumbs, you make out a blob in the dark. Wait, there are two blobs: some kind of rock, and beside it, a human. Or is it a shark?

'Amazing,' you say.

'You should try it. I can give you all the details of the place I went, if you like?'

'Thanks,' you say. You want to tell him that you have been here without going there — you have been to that dark, murky place where it's all too easy to mistake humans for sharks. Instead you just say, 'Maybe later.'

You return to your still too full inbox but make no headway with your attachments because your heart is whining to be heard. Alright, you tell it. And so you stand up and ask if anyone wants tea; of course, everyone does, and so, on the way to the kitchen, you distill your lightbulb moment into a text to your boyfriend.

At least, this is what you *think* you've texted him, until, just as your co-workers are complaining about your tea making skills yet again — *are you this bad on purpose? So we'll never ask you to make tea again?! Too weak, too strong, too much sugar, too milky* — your phone vibrates across your desk and when you open the message it says: LOL. WTF?

Not even bothering to defend your tea-making powers because so what if you die as a crap tea-maker, there are worse things, many worse things, you scroll back to what you thought was your genius message: I WRAP SWINE IN DEAL BUT WANT OK DONNY THING DEATH?

Oh God.

You text back: LOL. SORRY. WILL EXPLAIN LATER.

But as you delete unnecessary attachment after unnecessary attachment, you know that so much will have been thought and said and felt and seen and wondered and laughed about by the both of you come *later*, that you will forget to divulge the true meaning of your cryptic mid-morning text. But hey, maybe this is alright, too.

mix up

When they told me, *we'll make great TV from your story*, I thought: at last, I'll be that firework. I'll be that firework on Channel 4 with all the adverts in between, just like every other person in the UK wants to be. But my daughter said, 'Look, I don't even get why they'd want to make a programme about you, but whatever it is, be careful. Have you seen these programmes? They're essentially freak shows.'

'Yeah,' said my son to my daughter. 'A *freak* show. *Essentially* where you belong.'

She throws his iPad, he kicks her iPhone; finally, they're waging war with their bodies and I'm so caught up in my UN peacekeeping mission to pull them apart, I forget what I already know — that my daughter knows sense.

Whey they say, *this is your story*, and they hand me the remote and my story fills the small dark preview room two months before the rest of the UK sees it on TV, I tell them it's wrong. They've mixed up my story with someone else's story. *Oh*, they say, pushing a plate of custard creams toward me as if custard creams will make me see the world with happy, custardy eyes, *but this is what you told us. Word for word. The advert, the capture, the truck, the sexual slavery —*

ENOUGH, I tell them. I made a mistake in letting you make my story. *Oh*. They made sad faces at the custard creams. *That's a shame*, they say, before telling me, in that upside-down English way, that I've already signed away the rights to my story, this preview was just a courtesy, *terribly sorry for your misunderstanding but it is a rather thrilling production wouldn't you agree?*

When the story was finally on TV, my daughter invited all our friends and their dogs and their cats and their goldfish and their children, etc., to watch it in our sitting room. There were people all over the carpet and the sofa and the table and the walls — 'This is a real sitting room now,' my son joked. 'Ha, ha!' My daughter rushed back and forth to the kitchen with plastic plates of popcorn and plastic cups of Coke, and everyone said thank you thank you oh thanks so much, and my son was making everyone laugh, and I thought, maybe this isn't such a bad idea.

When the advert for the washing powder that would make you punch the air in time to a too-happy song was over, my story began, and every surface of our sitting room shut up. They even stopped sipping Coke and munching popcorn. *They took me from a dark place*, said a voice meant to be me, *and into a darker one. And I knew things would get darker, still, before I fought my way into the light*. Bad thing after bad thing happened to this girl; looking at the faces in our sitting rooms. They were so scared, they couldn't move, couldn't fart, didn't dare to look at me, and I thought, maybe they're scared that if they look, the bad things will happen to them too, and then I remembered this is why I act like my past is no darker than anybody else's. Then the sitting room blurred over as if there was a problem with the reception and maybe there was. Or maybe I was crying.

When the TV story was over and the advert woman was again punching the air in joy at her new washing powder, no one said anything. Then my son said: 'Now I get why you're so weird.'

And my daughter: 'Why didn't you tell us?'

My only answer was to squeeze their hands. The light and the dark were all mixed up and maybe this wasn't so bad. Maybe, one day soon, this would be okay. I squeezed and I squeezed until my daughter said ouch and pulled away. Then she stood up. She raised her plastic cup high over her head. 'A toast,' she said. 'To my mother, who has been through more than most of us could ever imagine and is all the more brilliant and crazy for it.'

And everyone struggled to their feet and they raised their plastic cups, and even though the Coke was a bit flat, they did drink.

London is a city of trying.

Trying to be faster, funnier, quirkier, cleverer; better at saving the world; or saving the pennies of the bank accounts of companies that are guzzling the world's rainforests faster than you, even with your boss breathing her coconut water breath down your neck, can type; better at persuading Groupon subscribers to buy more deals. You have tried at some of these things, but mostly, you are trying to live. You are trying to really be here, not just exist.

But trying is hard.

It's hard when you accidentally brush shoulders with a man on the way to work and he looks at you as if you don't have a right to exist, and that voice which lives in the part of you where no light ever gets, snarls, *See? Told you I was right*.

It's hard when an email pings into your inbox: *We regret to inform you that on this occasion. Or: ! IMPORTANT: Why is the Report File - Final 21.3 empty?*

It's hard when, on your millionth checking at what the screen tells you is 2:03 a.m., you admit it: that person is never going to text you back.

It's hard when one of your friends is on a 5:2 diet whilst everyone in your office is competing to see who can last the longest on protein shakes and lemon water; when you see maybe 25 images a day of women whose bodies resemble yours at your furthest-away-from-life-est, bodies which apparently help sell everything from sun cream to cinema tickets to pizza; when those who know give you the once over and tell you you're looking 'healthy' and when those who don't say 'Ohmygodyouresoluckyyouresotinyandye-tyoueatwhateveryouwant!'

It's hard to keep your unwelcome troglodyte companion from whispering in your (and only your) ear: *you are too big too loud too naughty too lazy and NEVER EVER GOOD ENOUGH.*

It's hard when you've just been dumped and when you're comfortably single and when you're so comfortable in your relationship that you don't always remember to shut the door when you go to the toilet.

It's hard being human; ordinary; freakish; a being with volume and weight; an interminably messy creature; a body which wants things; and a soul whose hunger, it seems, the harder you look up and down and under and over and around and around and through and in the cracks of this city, is never sated.

more than lunch

'What's so funny?' your husband asks, reading in your face the possibility of a laugh before you yourself realised it was there. 'You've got that look. Like you're about to make mischief.'

'Oh,' you say, 'well I used to…' You are about to tell him that you used to spend the best, and often the worst, part of every weekend in this car park through which the two of you, and your husband's parents and your daughter, are now walking. You are about to describe the soap factory that stood where your car is now parked, and how, when you were really high, you were like totally certain you could smell the ghost soap. You are about to introduce him to this other person you were before the two of you met. You've been meaning to do it ever since, but there was the marriage to think about, and then you got pregnant, and then you had to find a house, and then there were a million things to do to the house and, fuck… How did you get here?

You look around, in search of that young woman who didn't want to be an adult or a child, but some impossible nowhere thing; instead, you see another tired mother yelling at her boy to stop riding his micro-scooter between the cars. This woman's face manages to be bright red and blue-white at the same time and you know the feeling: drained to the bone yet puffed up on things to do, to do, to do, to do, to do…

Your husband grabs your arm and squeezes that bit too hard, as if he knows you are slipping away. 'Where's Hailey?'

'Isn't she with your parents?'

You both turn back to see his parents fussing over his dad's new camera, but no Hailey.

No Hailey. Your stomach drops down to your legs.

'You said she was with them!' you say.

'No, you said you'd watch her!' he says.

Six years and nine, no, ten months. For six years and ten months you have lived in fear of this crack — this bottomless crack in the universe. 'HAILEY!'

You leapfrog and crawl and duck between cars. All you see are stones, leaves, the occasional dog shit. The thought crosses your mind that this is some kind of divine punishment for your wanton past life; you dismiss this as bullshit Catholic guilt and try to remember that zen thing you read in that 'mindfulness for mummies' blog about imagining dark thoughts as passing clouds. This strikes you as bullshit, too.

'What on earth are you two up to?' laughs your mother-in-law. 'You look bonkers.' Your father-in-law is taking photographs of parked cars. Photographs of parked cars! You could slap him.

'Hailey,' you gasp. 'She's missing.'

'Oh,' your mother-in-law paws the air, 'She wanted to run ahead and play in that tunnel so I said sure.'

Your face does all the talking: what the fuck?

'For goodness sake,' she says, 'kids need a little freedom.'

'Sure.' you say, 'Right.'

'I told you we shouldn't have let them babysit,' you whisper to your husband, 'they're irresponsible.'

'Listen to you!' he exclaims. 'You're always having a go at them for being uptight. Looks like the tables have turned now, eh?'

Just then you see the tiny sillouette that is unmistakably your daughter's and you wonder — although of course you would never give him the satisfaction of saying this out loud — whether he's right.

Your daughter is squatting in the railway tunnel where you used to pick up, skin up and get stoned out of your mind. Used to grab fags, snogs, blow jobs, shags, the occasional stick of someone else's lipstick, away from the rain. And it still smells of these things — especially of the rain.

You squat down beside your daughter. 'What are you looking at?'

'I think it's Cinderella's shoe!' It is in fact a hideous once-white-now-brown fake-leather stiletto. 'I think she was rushing for the pumpkin and her shoe fell off but she didn't have time to go back for it. It's annoying about the pumpkin.'

You laugh. 'Something like that.'

'Oh do come on,' says your mother-in-Law. 'Our booking is for 1.00 and it's already 12.55. This is a very popular spot for Sunday lunch.'

'Coming,' you say, but you squat with your daughter a moment longer. She is only six, but already you can see it — the hunger in her eyes for something more than Sunday lunch. And maybe, you think, dragging her away from the filthy remains of a night out for which some stranger is right now paying a heavy price — maybe this isn't such a bad thing at all.

the engine

We have looked under paving stones and round the backs of banks whose money has long since run out.

We have looked on the moor and in your ear and in the stomach of a rare species of anteater found only in certain parts of the Amazon jungle on certain days of the week.

We have emailed a Survey Monkey to 1.3 million people; it remains unopened in 87% of their 'promotions' folders. We need to redesign the survey so that more people open it; a good idea would be to include an incentive for completion, e.g. half price at Pizza Express.

We don't know why people do things they know to be against their self-interest, e.g. smoke, buy scratch cards, stay married to people they hate, bully people they love, say yes when their body is saying no, and no when their heart is yelling yes yes YES.

We don't know why that man gave us such a filthy look when we accidentally bumped into him on the way to work this morning.

We don't know what it is our boss has booked the third best meeting room to talk to us about tomorrow afternoon.

We don't know why, sometimes, late at night, we feel as if there is a hole at the centre of everything; yes, there is a hole at the centre of everything, and we're falling into it, deeper and deeper every day. We don't know if anyone else feels like this or whether this hole is the dark matter that holds the universe together, or are we just a bit fucked up, who knows.

We don't know why some days are twice as long as others, and others ten times as heavy as the rest. We don't know why we slept with that person then spent the next day in a shopping centre whose bright lights and elbowing crowds and bad R&B made us feel even worse than remembering that we just slept with that person we didn't want to sleep with and don't even like. We don't know why we believed that £175 ill-fitting shoes would solve any of this.

We don't know why we can't quite be friends with our brother-in-law.

We don't know how it felt to be us at the age of three or what age we'll be when we die, or how it will feel, or whether we will feel it at all. We will die, though; all of us in this room, we are going to die. Occasionally, we can hold this end just out of sight, but close enough that it casts a shadow which makes us smile and laugh in wonder at the same old grey sky; yes, once or twice a month perhaps, we fizz with wonder. Yet mostly, we sink into the hot crowded cupboard of now, where we stamp and grunt when the train is four minutes late or when we spill wine on the freshly-ironed trousers which until a few seconds ago were beige.

We don't know how much we don't know. What we do know is this: it is the not knowing that drives us. On and on and on and on and on it drives, we hope it will never run out.

everything i know about divine light

1. Whilst their contemporaries were fighting for or against Communism, for or against Feminism, for or against a Mortgage and a Career, my parents were eating lentils and meditating and giving a proportion of their earnings to a fat little Indian boy they believed to be the source of Divine Light.

2. My mum was once arrested in Leeds for selling *The Divine Times*. She showed me the exact spot the second-to-last time she visited me; it was now occupied by a busker, who was singing a particularly angsty version of 'Hey Jude' which, judging by the paucity of coppers in his guitar case, was bringing the people of Leeds less light than the shopping centres which overlooked him on all sides.

3. My dad is now an atheist. If you're thinking of bringing up Divine Light when he's around, don't. Mind you, if you talk about the weather, or what you did over the weekend, or the traffic, or that thing you read about that terrible thing that happened in that other country in the paper, or your new shoes, he will find a way, with mysterious regularity, to link it to that unmentionable topic. *All those years, all that money, all my life, devoted to something which wasn't real, which was*

worse... I never know how to reply to such talk, so I don't. I'm lucky if such a conversation coincides with his weekly visit from Bob and Samuel, two Jehovah's Witnesses, who he invites into his house every week in the hope of convincing them they are wrong.

4. My mum says that if it hadn't been Divine Light, it would have been something worse. It would have been drugs. It would have been scars and clinics and highs and lows and the gutter. By that standard, lentils and meditation were not so bad. These days, she eats less lentils, more tofu. *And it's such a beautiful idea, don't you think?* she might say, after her after-work glass of wine. *The idea of bringing divine light, eternal peace and calmness, to every person all over the world.*

5. Every time I try to meditate, I either a) Worry about all the things I ought to be doing instead of meditating, then start worrying about the fact that I am worrying about these things when I ought to be meditating; finally I worry that the fact that I'm worrying about the fact that I'm worrying when I'm meant to be meditating means that there is something wrong with me, i.e. maybe I'm destined for a life of eternal anti-calm. Or b) I fall asleep, only to wake a few moments later, stiff and pissed off.

6. Now, when my parents, who are long-since divorced, start shouting — they have to shout because they are both quite

deaf and hate wearing their hearing aids — about this or that person they knew from their Divine Light days, about this or that scandal that has since emerged, I bury their words in the electric glow of my Smartphone. How I managed before Smartphones, I don't remember.

7. When I was a little girl, I used to watch my dad watch videos of the little fat Indian boy who was meant to be the bringer of Divine Light. In these videos the boy on stage blinked and smiled at unbelievably huge crowds. I remember asking my dad how comes he was a bringer of light. My dad said because his dad was, and then his dad died, and I remember feeling less jealous of the boy and more sad, because he was littler than I was, and he didn't even have a dad. But I was a bit jealous: it would be nice, I thought, if I didn't have to make and do and say things, and if these things didn't have to be as close to perfect as possible, in order to be watched. It would be nice for people to love you just for being here, in the world, sitting down, doing nothing.

8. My dad's family are Jewish, my mum's are lapsed Anglican. Neither of them mention my parents' time with The Divine Light. On the rare occasion they do, they skate over it as quickly as possible, asking instead, about my time at Oxford, or that award I won, and I open my mouth and tell them everything they want to hear, about the gowns and the essays and other Impressive Things which I've pursued the

way my parents pursued The Light, and even though they murmur praise, even though they are watching and smiling and isn't this all I wanted, for people to watch and smile and think me special, the buzz is already wearing off; the real me is slipping into the gaps between these words, so many gaps, for example, the thing each Impressive Thing is an attempt to run away from, i.e. the fact that I wouldn't be here, had my parents not found in each other in their search for a light which has not only turned out to be less than divine, but has, in the highest echelons of its organisational structures, aided corruption and — so my dad likes to remind me whilst I'm busy Liking a Facebook rant about how annoying those *lose 10lbs of belly flab in 10 days* ads are — child abuse.

9. On a street very near the street where my mum was arrested and where I now live, Jehovah Witnesses stand every day, in the rain, the sun, the sleet, and that mean, mean wind that I'm pretty sure is unique to Leeds, brandishing smiles that stretch from earlobe to earlobe and such soul-twanging questions as: WHAT IS TRUE HAPPINESS? And: IS SATAN REAL? Most of the time I pretend not to see them, but other times, I look them in the eye and I laugh.

10. If I believe in anything, I believe that no matter how many times we sand the pavement, no matter how many books we read or sit-ups we do, there will always be cracks, and we, whether we're using our GPS or our A to

Z or one of those silly cartoon tourist maps or one of those Boris bike maps, whether we're following our instincts, a best friend, a stranger, a lover or a mother, we will fall into them. We'll skin our chins and our noses. We'll tear our new jeans. Some people will step over us, others will laugh, and maybe, if we're very lucky, some might take a few seconds out of the day they've got planned, that perfect day forever shimmering on the horizon, and help us up. Most of the time, however, it's up to us to move and scream and shout — whatever it takes to find the voice that will get us out.

acknowledgements

Thanks Leeds City Council and the Arts Council England for funding me to make a live art installation at Leeds Light Night 2014, which is where many of these stories were born.

Thank you to all my friends and family for providing me with light, dark and many other essentials, even — perhaps especially — when you didn't know you were doing it; most particularly, thank you Anna, for showing me what I needed to be shown about the cracks.

Thank you, David.

Thank you Kit Caless for your enthusiastic and thoughtful response to this collection; thanks, too, Gary Budden and Sanya Semakula for your hard work behind the scenes.

Nb. This book was made possible by the continuing uplift of our lifetime supporters, Bob West and Barbara Richards.

ALSO AVAILABLE FROM 🔲 INFLUX PRESS

Attrib. and other stories
Eley Williams

'She is a writer for whom one struggles to find comparison, because she has arrived in a class of her own: witty, melancholy, occasionally sensual, occasionally mordant, elegantly droll. She has in common with George Saunders the ability to be both playful and profound, and we are lucky to have her.'
– Sarah Perry, author of *The Essex Serpent*

Attrib. and other stories celebrates the tricksiness of language just as it confronts its limits. Correspondingly, the stories are littered with the physical ephemera of language: dictionaries, dog-eared pages, bookmarks and old coffee stains on older books. This is writing that centres on the weird, tender intricacies of the everyday where characters vie to 'own' their words, tell tall tales and attempt to define their worlds.

With affectionate, irreverent and playful prose, the inability to communicate exactly what we mean dominates this bold debut collection from one of Britain's most original new writers.

ISBN: 978-1-910312-16-2

ALSO AVAILABLE FROM ⊠ INFLUX PRESS

Signal Failure
London to Birmingham, HS2 on Foot
Tom Jeffreys

'Through it all, Jeffreys's writing is intelligent, engaging and engaged, and deeply and disarmingly human.'
— *New Statesman*

One November morning, Tom Jeffreys set off from Euston Station with a gnarled old walking stick in his hand and an overloaded rucksack. His aim was to walk the 119 miles from London to Birmingham along the proposed route of HS2. Needless to say, he failed.

Over the course of ten days of walking, Jeffreys meets conservationists and museum directors, fiery farmers and suicidal retirees. From a rapidly changing London, through interminable suburbia, and out into the English countryside, Jeffreys goes wild camping in Perivale, flees murderous horses in Oxfordshire, and gets lost in a landfill site in Buckinghamshire.

ISBN: 978-1-910312-14-8

ALSO AVAILABLE FROM ✕ INFLUX PRESS

Above Sugar Hill
Linda Mannheim

'Mannheim's restive tales of her desiccated stretch of New York provoke and abide like a slap.'
– Eimear McBride, author of *A Girl is a Half-Formed Thing*

'Smouldering vignettes of New York life are both achingly sad and beautifully wrought. These are stories to savour.'
– Stuart Evers

An unforgettable collection of short stories set in Washington Heights, New York City. .

These tales of New York take place between 1973 and 2001 – a Puerto Rican Independentista fends off the FBI, a young girl spots Marilyn Monroe more than ten years after Monroe's suicide, an opera-singing housing activist goes missing and presumed to have been murdered. Above Sugar Hill is a literary map of Upper Manhattan, uncompromising narratives and complicated truths.

ISBN: 978-0-9927655-2-1

INFLUX
PRESS

Influx Press is an independent publisher based in London, committed to publishing innovative and challenging fiction, poetry and creative non-fiction from across the UK and beyond. We find stories from the margins of culture, specific geographical spaces, sites of resistance and bold experiments that remain under explored in mainstream literature.

www.influxpress.com

@Influxpress